An Empty Chair

About *Diffodd y Sêr*, the Welsh-language original version of this novel:

'Writing about one of humanity's ugliest events is not an easy task for an author, but Haf Llewelyn succeeds. Nothing is held back. But alongside shocking descriptions there are sensitive and profound passages, and the author succeeds in bringing elements of happiness and some lightness to the lives of her characters.'

Menna Lloyd Williams, former Head of Children's Fiction, Welsh Books Council

'Good to see an author who doesn't dilute a story by assuming that children are too young to understand some things. Children can often understand better than adults. I believe that this is a novel which people of all ages will find worth reading.'

Helen Angharad Evans, *Barn*

The story of Welsh
First World War
poet Hedd Wyn

An Empty
Chair

H A F L L E W E L Y N

First impression: 2017
© Haf Llewelyn & Y Lolfa Cyf., 2017

Cover design: Y Lolfa
Cover illustration: Iola Edwards
Translation of Hedd Wyn's 'Gwenfron and I' by Howard Huws

ISBN: 978 1 78461 452 2

The publishers wish to acknowledge the support of
Cyngor Llyfrau Cymru

Published and printed in Wales
on paper from well-maintained forests by
Y Lolfa Cyf., Talybont, Ceredigion SY24 5HE
e-mail ylolfa@ylolfa.com
website www.ylolfa.com
tel 01970 832 304
fax 832 782

Foreword

Farmer's son Ellis Humphrey Evans was born in the village of Trawsfynydd in North Wales in 1887. Although he left school at an early age to start work as a shepherd on the family farm, he was soon winning prizes for his poetry both locally and further afield, and was awarded the bardic name Hedd Wyn ('Blessed Peace'). This novel takes a fresh look at one of the most famous stories in the history of Welsh poetry: that of the Eisteddfod of the Black Chair – the National Eisteddfod of 1917, held in Birkenhead against the backdrop of the slaughter in the trenches of the First World War.

Diffodd y Sêr, Haf Llewelyn's original Welsh-language version of this novel, won the prize for the 'Secondary' category in the prestigious Tir na-nOg awards for children's fiction in 2014, and is already a modern classic taught on the Welsh Literature GCSE syllabus.

Notes on Welsh language and culture

awdl
ode – a long poem in strict meter

bach (_fach_ after a female name)
This literally means _small_, but it's also used as a term of affection.

Band o'Hope
The temperance movement, which warned about the problems that drinking alcohol could cause and encouraged people not to, was very popular in this period. Band o'Hope was a national children's organisation founded in 1847 to promote these ideas.

hwyl
fun

nain
gran/grandma

National Eisteddfod (plural: Eisteddfodau)
Annual competitive arts festival held entirely in Welsh, and the most important Welsh-language cultural event of the year. It includes competitions for poetry, prose, singing, dancing, art, drama and many other things. The location for the National Eisteddfod changes each year, and though now it alternates

between North and South Wales, in 1917 it was held in Birkenhead, near Liverpool. The Chair is the most important and prestigious prize of all, and it's awarded to the poet who writes the best long poem in strict meter. The winner is enthroned on the Chair in a special ceremony called the Chairing of the Bard. Smaller local eisteddfodau are also held in many towns and villages.

snichyn
snitch, sneak, little rat

sol-fa
An old system used to teach people to sing or play instruments, where the notes are given names (*do, re, mi* etc).

tada
dad

taid
grandad

temperance vow / pledge
A formal promise people made never to drink alcohol.

y / yr
the

ych a fi!
yuk!

Acknowledgements

I would like to sincerely thank Y Lolfa for the opportunity to reach new audiences with my novel *Diffodd y Sêr* through the publication of this English adaptation.

A very special thanks to the editor, Carolyn Hodges, for her advice, thoroughness and wise words. Thank you to the Welsh Books Council for their support. Thank you to Howard Huws for permission to reproduce his beautiful translation of 'Gwenfron and I'. And thank you again to all at Yr Ysgwrn for their continued warm welcome – *diolch yn fawr*.

Haf Llewelyn
July 2017

1

'No, he's not on his way home, Lora – it's not true. It can't be true, and your mam didn't get a telegram,' Wil Ferret sticks his thin little nose in the air. 'My mam would know if your tada was on the way home, 'cos your mam tells my mam everything, so there.'

'It's the truth, I'm telling you – it *is* true!' wails Lora, pleading with me. Lora's my best friend, and best friends should always stick together.

'But are you sure?' I blurt, and wish instantly that I'd kept my mouth shut tight, as tight as Wil's fist.

'Of course I'm sure! A telegram arrived this morning for Mam.' Lora looks at me, her head tilted, eyes blistering – *you traitor,* they say.

'Is he coming home, Lora? Really coming home?' Lora nods, and her eyes soften. *Go on Annie, tell him – just tell Wil Ferret that he doesn't know anything, and that's he's a little* snichyn.

But I stand there, silently looking from Lora to Wil, and from Wil to Lora. What should I say? I kick at a bit of loose turf, scuffing the polish off my best shoes. Wil Ferret fills me with dread, but Lora's my best friend... I should be on her side, of course I should, but I can't challenge Wil Ferret.

'He won't be coming home until the war's over, so you're telling lies, Lora. Big fat lies.' He pushes his face close to Lora's and jabs his finger in the air with every word. 'Big – Fat – Lies!'

Wil knows about these matters – he knows about the war. 'Our boys will be there until the end,' he adds. 'Right till the end – our boys will be there to beat the Hun, and then perhaps your tada can come home, Lora. It's Lloyd George you see, he's the boss and we have to do *exactly* as Lloyd George says. And when I'm old enough, I'll be there giving those Huns what for. *Rat-tat-tat!*

Bullets of loose chippings scatter around our feet as Wil jumps to face a whole battalion of imaginary troops approaching from behind the school gate. Wil's like that – he's got too many pictures in his head.

Lora rushes past me and makes off down the path, her face a dangerous shade of scarlet, all puckered up. When she's angry, she does that – she twists her face into the most unexpected shapes, her eyes all screwed up until her nose is almost flat, her cheeks sucked in. The other boys have joined Wil in his shooting game.

'Hey, look boys! Lora's got her pig face on!' he shouts, letting the imaginary Lee-Enfield drop to his feet.

'Oink, oink, Lora!' There he is, snorting, mimicking a pig, and all the boys laughing and pointing at my best friend, pelting each other with pine cones and chanting 'Oink, oink, Lora – pig face Lora.'

Do something Anni, the voice inside my head's shouting. *Go on, Annie, do something – she's your best friend.* I should have said something, should have backed her story up, should have punched Wil's silly little nose. But I'd stood there saying nothing – what would my brother Ellis say if he found out that I'd let my best friend be humiliated by those stupid boys?

'Lora, wait for me!' The pine cones start pelting the back of my dress as I run down towards the bend in the road where Lora's disappeared. She's faster than me, and once she's got the huff, then that's that – she won't stop, she keeps on running. I'm cross now. I hadn't really questioned or doubted her story, I just asked if she was sure – but I'm cross with myself more than I'm cross with Lora. I know Lora like... well, I know her like I know of all the twists and turns that are on this path now. She's impatient, she'll jump down your throat one minute and hug you the next – that's Lora, my best friend. And best friends never doubt each other, do they?

'Lora, wait!' But she hasn't waited for me – she isn't there waiting when I reach the little rock that sticks out into the path. I stop running. I shouldn't be running anyway, because I've just recovered from the cough, and if Mam knew I was running and becoming breathless and huffing like this, she'd make me go straight back to bed, and wrap that goosy smelly cloth around my throat again. I retch just thinking about it.

So I slow down and start kicking more stones on the path. How stupid I was to doubt Lora Margaret, my best friend. If Lora says there was a telegram for her mam this morning, then there *was* a telegram for her mam, and that's that.

The black blanket's starting to wrap itself around me now – the one that comes when I'm sad. It's tangible, so real that I almost stumble in its folds when I reach the stile, and try to lift my foot on to the first step. That's when I see her, sitting all hunched up on the other side of the stone wall.

'It's me, Lora,' I whisper, and sit there on the top step. I know she's crying because her breath comes in little tremors.

I put my hand in my pocket and feel the small quartz stone in my hand, cool and sharp. I spotted it this morning on the edge of the flower border, and I picked it up and put it in my pocket quickly, in case Mam saw me. I do that – when I see a quartz stone, I have to pick it up and keep it, because something tells me, a little voice in my head tells me that if I don't pick it up then something bad might happen. I know – it's silly, and I've promised Mam that I'll try not to do it, because she's had enough of mending my pockets.

I hold the stone in my hand, and study it. This is one of the best. It has veins of different colours running through it: purple and pink hues. I spit on it and rub at the dirt with my finger and thumb. It's a beautiful stone, a lucky one.

'Look what I found this morning.' I jump down and land with a thud beside Lora. I offer her the stone and she takes it. Her eyes are red. Her nose is red too, from all the rubbing that she's done, I suppose.

'Your nose is red, Lora,' I blurt out. 'It's because you've been rubbing it.' I can never stop myself from saying stupid things like that. Why have I said that now? But she just laughs, and I sit down beside her and hold on to her arm.

'I'm sorry, Lora. You know, for… well, for not bashing Wil on the nose. He's a right *snichyn*, nasty little rat.'

'It's pretty, Anni.' She turns the stone in her hand and studies it, raising it towards the light so that the sun can reach into the cracks. 'Where did you find it?'

'In the garden. Do you like it?'

'Yes, it's all shimmering light.' Then she places it on her finger as though it's a ring.

'Has Lloyd George got a son?' she asks.

'I don't know, Lora. He might have and he might be in France, just like your dad.'

'No.' She pushes her face towards the sun. 'He's the Prime Minister, Anni, and the sons of important people don't have to go to France, do they? Anyway, if he does have a son, then I'll marry him, and I'll have a ring with a stone as big as this one!'

I really can't see how it would be possible for Lora Margaret to marry the son of an important man like Lloyd George, but I keep my mouth shut this time, tightly shut. Ellis says that everyone has a right to dream, to hope, and to have aspirations.

'When did you find the stone, Anni?' she asks, her eyes suddenly bright and clear.

'This morning, why?'

'This morning? That's when Mam had the telegram, then.' She reaches out, placing the stone in my hand. She's smiling.

'It's a lucky stone, Anni. Keep it safely.'

I put it back in my pocket, and push it into the lining. Mam won't find it there.

'That's strange,' I say, and take Lora's arm. 'But you're right, it must bring luck.'

Just then a thought pings into my head.

'Lora,' I whisper, 'when you marry Lloyd George's son... can I be your bridesmaid, and can I have flowers in my hair... real silk flowers?'

She nods, straightens, tightens her grip on my arm, and we walk elegantly down the aisle in the chapel, until we reach the road. And all is well, because I will be the main bridesmaid in the wedding of Lora and the eldest son of David Lloyd George.

2

As I RUSH up the road towards Yr Ysgwrn, my home, I realise that I haven't asked Lora properly about the telegram. I haven't had a chance, and that's Wil Ferret's fault of course, because he's just a little *snichyn*, questioning Lora like that.

Will Lora's mam be pleased about the telegram, I wonder? I think of turning back towards the village, but it's getting late and Mam will be worried. As I reach the front porch, I sense that someone other than Mam is there. I fling the door open, and Gwen Jones is sitting there in the kitchen, by the table – rod straight – one of Mam's Sunday cups in her scrawny hand.

'Well, at least he's one of the lucky ones,' she says, her fingers clutching the dainty teacup as if she expects it to crack and crumble between her fingers. 'He's coming home you see, that's the talk. Coming home... very lucky *indeed*.' The silver spoon jumps as she roughly places the cup on to the saucer. I look at Mam: these are her best cups – we never let them drop on to the saucer like that.

Mam shoots me a warning look.

'Lucky?' Mam's voice is quiet and strained. 'Do you think so, Gwen? I'm not sure that I'd call him one of the lucky ones. Will you have some more tea...?'

She nods towards me, as if to tell Gwen Jones that the conversation is over. Whatever the topic, it's not for my ears. That's silly: I'm almost 14, but they still talk in whispers when they want to discuss certain matters. But I know about the war and that, so I don't know why they won't let me in on their conversations. Anyway, Mam turns and gives me a quizzical look.

She knows I've been running because the heat in the kitchen's making my cheeks burn.

'Anni – at last! Where have you been…?' she asks, her voice strange, her words coming too quickly. She's got something up her sleeve that she doesn't want me to know about. 'Have you been fooling around with those lads again?'

'No!' What does she mean? I never fool around with the boys down by the Forge, they're all silly and irritating – Wil the worst of them, of course. What's made Mam say such a thing, with Gwen Jones sitting there?

'No, I walked home with Lora,' I gasp, knowing that I shouldn't answer Mam back like that, especially as Gwen Jones is there, sitting like the Queen of Sheba.

'You walked home with Lora?' Gwen Jones turns her gaze at me and sniffs, as if I've brought in something *ych-a-fi* on the bottom of my shoe.

'And how was Lora Margaret today?' she asks. I shudder. I hate it when Gwen Jones comes to visit. She always has that stiff black dress on, her narrow neck poking out of the lace collar, and the fur with the head of a small fox at the end draped around her shoulders. It looks as if the fox is alive and afraid of sliding off her skinny frame.

Mam has a fur stole, and I rather like it. It's a warm, reddish colour. Mam hardly ever wears it, she keeps it wrapped in tissue paper up in her bedroom. She wore it for Uncle Robert's wedding, and now Maggie has it, as she's gone to Liverpool for a few days to visit our other sisters. Sometimes Enid, my youngest sister, and I go upstairs and play at being 'ladies' with Mam's stole. Mam's fur stole is lovely and soft, and nothing like this ugly creature clinging on to Gwen Jones's shoulders, its hard, frozen eyes watching my every move.

'And how was Lora Margaret today?' The question hangs. Mam turns to face me, urging me on.

'Anni, Mrs Jones has asked you a question.'

I have to be careful: Gwen Jones is a word thief. She can steal words from your mouth without you realising it. Just half a word will be seized as it leaves your lips – stolen, twisted and stretched. How can I answer? If I say Lora's 'well, thank you,' then she'll twist even those few innocent words, and report back to Aunty Kitty, Lora's mam, that I said that Lora was only just 'well'. So I pause, until my mam's eyes force me to say something.

'Lora was fine, thank you, Mrs Jones.' I congratulate myself – there, just safe words, she can do no harm with those. Mam lets out a sigh and goes through to the scullery to fetch some milk, so she doesn't hear Gwen Jones's next words.

'She should be better than "just fine", what with her father coming home.'

The hard, frozen eyes of the fox bore into me, my cheeks burning. So it's true: Lora's father *is* coming home, and I should have known. I should have known because I'm Lora's best friend – I should know these things. I bend my face, and concentrate on chewing my bread and butter. I can't swallow, it'll get stuck in my throat.

'Lora should be better than just fine, she should be delighted – her father coming home from France, all dandy and well, I bet, and my Ben having to stay there. It's fine for those who are lucky enough.'

Mam's back from the scullery. I can see from her face that she's bracing herself. She knows what will follow – we both know what's coming. I want to go to her. I want to stand by her, stand between Mam and Mrs Jones's words.

'And then there are those fit young men who don't have to go to France at all, and lord it around here without a care in the world, writing their poetry and showing off at the eisteddfodau while my Ben's away fighting their battles.'

Just then I hear the men coming through the gate into the

yard – my father, with my brothers Ellis, Ifan and Bob. They've been down on the low fields digging ditches all day. They'll be famished by now. I can hear their voices: high pitched, laughing at something that Ellis has said, all in good spirits.

Doors, it comes to me, are clever inventions. Either side of this door, this piece of wood, there are two different worlds, two opposing universes, and they are about to clash. On this side with the fire glowing on the hearth, Mam, Gwen Jones and myself sit, and I'm stone: solid, cold. Out there in the wind, I can feel the warmth of the men as they banter. I concentrate hard: I must use all my will to make that door stay shut. Please don't open, I say over and over and over. Please don't open.

It works. I can hear the men passing on to the back room to change out of their sodden clothes.

Mam gets up and almost skips to the scullery. She comes back with a jar of blackberry jam.

'Thank you for calling, Gwen,' she says as she hands over the jam, but I can tell she's not really thanking Gwen Jones for visiting us. Mam rarely says things she doesn't mean. Gwen Jones puts the jam in her basket and gets to her feet, making for the door. She grabs the hem of her black dress, as if she doesn't want it dirtied.

'I hope you have good news soon... about Ben and... I wish you well, Gwen.' But Gwen Jones has already crossed the threshold and I watch her as she picks her way down the path, the dead fox dangling from her shoulder, his eyes still watchful.

It's as if she's raised her stony finger and pointed it in Mam's face. It's Ellis, of course – he's still at home, working with Tada on the farm. Not like her son Ben, and the other young men – they've already enlisted, and the war's swallowed them up. We've still got Ellis, and I pray every night we can keep it that way.

All the papers say the war's going well, and our soldiers are the best there are, of course, so it won't be long now. But if all is going so well, I can't understand why they always seem to need more soldiers. I'm not sure what to believe, but Lora says one of my brothers will have to go sooner or later, and I push the thought to the shadowy part of my mind. I try not to dwell on that. Ellis is the eldest, and he's almost 30 now – getting on – and soon Bob will be 18, so there'll be two men of enlisting age at Yr Ysgwrn.

I don't think we'll have a cake to celebrate when Bob turns 18, somehow. I know Mam's dreading that day. Then there's Ifan, who's 15, and he's strong – although I'd never tell him that, of course, because he's always bragging about something or other. And then there's Tada, but he's too old to fight, and he has creaky legs. Some days he can hardly straighten. He'd never be able to work the farm, he could never get the ploughing done, without my brothers' help. But I've heard of the tribunals, and how hard they are – they won't take any notice of Tada's arthritis or realise that he needs lots of help. I don't want Tada to go to any tribunal – it wouldn't be right, not Tada.

So I suppose Lora's right: Ellis or Bob will have to go – it's the law. I can't see Ellis as a soldier. He's a dreamer, a poet; he's forever writing silly little rhymes to entertain Enid and me. Sometimes they're cheeky, and we have to hide them or Mam would tell us all off. But mostly his poems are beautiful, and he always wins at the local eisteddfodau. Anyway, Ellis wouldn't know what to do with a bayonet or rifle, or whatever weapons they've got there in France. He'd probably miss the target, or shoot the wrong people.

Why can't this stupid war end? It makes everyone sad. There's always a sigh in the air these days.

I help Mam clear the Sunday cups away. She's quiet. I really hate Gwen Jones, and I know that hating anyone is a sin, but there you are. I want to rush out after her and scream at the old witch. I don't know what to say to try and comfort Mam... I touch her shoulder lightly and she turns to look at me, and tries to smile, but I know she wants to cry. But mothers don't cry.

'Don't take any notice of her,' she says, but of course I can't ignore Gwen Jones's words, they're stuck in my head. I should be able to comfort Mam, but I can only ask,

'Do you think that Ellis will have to go?'

Mam takes one look towards the form, the tribunal form, stuck there between the jugs on the dresser.

'We'll wait and see what they say at the next tribunal – don't go looking for worry, Anni. And don't say a word about Gwen Jones now, when Ellis comes in.'

We busy ourselves getting tea ready, and I change out of my shoes and put on my work clogs. It's my job to fetch water. I can hear Bob and Ifan talking as they're feeding the horses.

'Careful with the water, Anni – don't go spilling it all over the place, it's already muddy out there.' Tada passes me on his way in. I nod. I made a real mess this morning, but I almost give Ellis away by giggling as he mimics Tada, making a grave face and wagging his finger in front of my nose.

At the well I fill the buckets, and watch for a moment as the clouds form thin, wispy ribbons away over the mountains, towards the sea. I watch as they change colours, weaving pink, crimson and yellow threads of shimmering silk across the sky. That's where the sea is, the other side of the mountains, and Ellis has promised he'll take us there – Enid and me. He's going to take us to Barmouth on the train, and Maggie says she'll come too if Mam's happy about it. Maggie went there once on a Sunday School trip. Barmouth's a remarkable place, full of grand shops, donkey rides on the front, and visitors from England paddling in the sea.

I clutch both bucket handles, but I'm still watching the clouds, so I'm not looking where my clogs are going. That's when one of the buckets slips and water spills over my feet

– cold, freezing water. The thought of the warm seawater at Barmouth disappears as the colours slide from the sky. I put the buckets away under the slate shelf in the scullery, take my clogs off, and carry them into the kitchen. Mam would have noticed the muddy clogs if it had been an ordinary day, but as soon as I come into the kitchen, I know.

Mam stands leaning on the table, her face pinched. Everyone else sits in silence.

Ellis and Tada are sitting at the table, their untouched tea in front of them.

'When?' Tada asks.

'Tomorrow.' Ellis has his head bowed. Mam sighs and lowers herself down heavily on to the stool by the hearth.

'Wait until next week, Ellis, give yourself time to think it over...' she tries, weakly.

'I've done nothing but think of it, Mam, for days – weeks.'

'But you don't *have* to go!' She's begging him with her eyes, but his head remains bowed.

'Yes, I do, Mam.'

'No!'

She sits there on the stool, her whole body shuddering, trying to hide the tears. This is the first time I've ever seen my mother cry, and when I realise that, I'm not a child any more. When you stop being a child, you understand for the first time that mothers do cry. They're silent tears, tears that make everyone ache.

'We must let him decide, Mary,' says Tada, but he can't raise his head to meet our gaze.

That's when I know I have to do something, as I'm no longer a child.

'Ellis?' I want him to explain.

'I'm going to Ffestiniog tomorrow, to enlist,' is all he says. And that's when I join my mother on the hearth, and we cling to each other, weeping.

3

'MAM SAID I had to watch out for Jim, but I wanted to go with her to the hospital – I should have gone, you know, I could find the money for the ticket...'

I nod. I'm not really listening to Lora, because my head's full of Ellis dressed in his uniform. Not that he's got his uniform yet, but I can't get the picture out of my head.

I'm keeping Lora company, and helping her with her little brother Jim, because her mam's gone to visit Uncle Ifor, Lora's Tada – he's in a hospital somewhere along the coast, in a place called Conwy.

'Strange, Anni.'

'What?'

I wonder if Ellis will have to wear some other soldier's uniform? I shudder – perhaps they're given dead soldiers' uniforms, as long as they've died cleanly, not with blood everywhere. I feel sick.

'Strange that your Ellis is going off just as my tada's coming home,' Lora says.

'Yes, but is Uncle Ifor coming home – I mean, is your tada really coming home?' I shove my thoughts about uniforms away to the shady part of my brain.

'I hope so, because I've told Jim that his daddy's coming home soon.'

Lora sweeps Jim *bach* up into her arms, and hugs him tight. Jim's only five, the youngest of Lora's brothers, and we spoil him rotten. You really can't *but* spoil him: he looks just like the picture of the angel in chapel, with his tight blond curls and his eyes the colour of the sky on a haymaking day. But Jim doesn't talk like other children, he just smiles with his mouth open and Lora or Aunty Kitty has to wash and dress him each morning. I asked Mam once what five-year-old children should be able to do, because I couldn't bring myself to ask Lora somehow.

'What do you mean?' Mam looked at me. 'What makes you ask?'

'Jim's five now.'

'Ah! Bless him, the little one!' she said and smiled, 'I don't suppose he'll be like other children. Something went amiss when he was born, but Jim is, and always will be, very special – so he'll make it, and everyone will love him.'

And that's why Jim has a special place in a corner of my heart – I don't know where exactly, but I'll always look out for Jim, anyway. So Lora had to stay at home to look after Jim, and Aunty Kitty had to take the train to visit her husband on her own.

'What's wrong with your tada, Lora?' I hesitate – is it prying? I'm not sure if I really want to know, but then I am Lora's best friend.

I've heard of soldiers returning home with terrible wounds and injuries that make it impossible for them to stand, let alone stand and fight. I've heard of men with limbs twisted and maimed, men who can do nothing but sit and stare into grates, looking for flames to warm their missing legs. Then I remember the whispering between Tada and Mam. It was that man from Blaenau: Tada said that his mind had broken into little shards because of the months he'd spent in the trenches. I don't really know what Tada meant, so I ask Lora.

'Lora, say if your mind is broken, you know... what does it mean? What exactly would be wrong? You know, like that man from Blaenau?'

'He's doolally isn't he? You know – mad, not right in the head.' Lora can just say things – just sort it out verbally, like that.

'What *is* mad, though?' I need to understand this properly, just in case. In case Ellis... well, I can't think that, so I stop.

Lora's knotting my hair into a tight plait at the back of my head.

'When you're mad, then your mind's blown – you can't think properly.'

'Why, what does the man from Blaenau do, then?' I ask.

'He gets up in the dead of night, and goes out into the street screaming. My Aunty Jane lives next door to him, and she gets woken by him shouting, *'Over the top, lads, go on now, over the top...'* He does it all the time, and then his poor wife comes out and tries to coax him back in, and then he hides behind the clock with his hands over his head.'

'What does that mean, then?'

'What?' Lora looks puzzled.

'You know – the *'over the top'* bit?' I can ask Lora anything, especially English words. She's better than me with with English words, and she never laughs or makes out that I'm silly for not knowing things.

'Right!' She ties a ribbon to hold the plait in my hair, then she squats down with her hands over her head, 'The soldiers have to crouch like this, see, because if they stand up in the trench, then the Hun will shoot at them. Then, when the whistle sounds, they have to get up and scramble out of the trench, over the wire and on to no man's land – that's where the fighting happens.'

I'm not sure if Lora has it quite right there. I think that if you're in the trench, then you may be safe, but then Lora knows more about these things. That's when Jim joins us, so we all start jumping up and running around the kitchen, as if we're climbing out of the trench, *'over the top, lads... over the top, lads...'* Lora leads, *'otopads... otopads...'*, Jim chases us, dribbling all over his collar and making shooting noises, and we all end up rolling on the hearth laughing.

When we stop playing at being soldiers, we decide it's time for Jim's tea. The three of us sit by the table and I put a little blackberry jam on Jim's bread and butter. He sits there chewing noisily, and little rivulets of sticky purple drool run down his chin, so I take out my hanky to wipe them away. Angels don't have blackberry spit on their chins.

'What's wrong with him?' I ask Lora.

'What do you mean?' Lora looks at Jim and back at me – and then I realise what she's thinking.

'No – not Jim!' I blurt. 'What's wrong with your father?'

Lora smiles suddenly.

'I don't know, but we'll find out when Mam comes home. We only had a telegram to tell us that he was coming out of the army, you know. Telegrams don't say much.'

Lora picks Jim up and out of his chair, and he runs out to look for his brothers.

'You remember that day when I told you about the telegram to tell us he was coming home,' she starts.

'Yes and Wil Ferret, *y snichyn*, didn't believe you.' I hope she doesn't remember that I was slow to back her up.

'Well, it only told us Tada was out of the fighting, it didn't tell us he was hurt exactly. But he must be hurt, you see, Anni, otherwise he'd still be there, wouldn't he?'

Suddenly Lora looks so sad and worried that I have to say something.

'Perhaps... well, perhaps he's only hurt a little. You know, like Hywel Rhos's father. He just hurt his foot, didn't he...?'

Damn, I'll rot in Hell – why can't I shut my blabbing mouth? Gwen Jones says that Hywel Rhos's father shot himself in his own foot so that he could come home, and that he's a coward and a disgrace to himself and his family, and Gwen Jones knows *for sure*, because that's what cowards do. Gwen Jones says Hywel Rhos's father should go in front of a court martial for what he's done. I don't know what a court martial is, but I don't think it's anything like a Sunday School Committee – it's much more serious than that, but I know I shouldn't ask Lora.

'I don't think it's just his foot, Anni.' But Lora doesn't go on, she sits there quite still.

'That's good,' I say. 'He can always kick a ball about with Jim, then.'

We sit there not saying anything for a while, and I can hear Jim humming to himself just beyond the open door.

'I'm afraid, Anni. I think it's his head. Mam said something about his head being hurt, but she didn't know for certain.' Then she looks up, her eyes filling. 'What if he's doolally, Anni – you know, like that man from Blaenau. What if he's not... you know, what if he's not the same Tada as he was before he went away?'

She's crying, but not making a noise. The tears just keep on rolling, and she just lets them. I hate this bloody war. I take out my hanky – it has purple streaks on it, but its lace is still lovely. Ellis bought me and Mam and Enid a hanky each when he went to Ffestiniog to put his name down.

'There.' I give it to Lora to wipe away her tears. 'You can keep it.'

Why did I say that? I'd meant to keep it safely as a token of luck that Ellis would return safely from the war. But now I've given it, I can't ask for it back. Decent people don't do that kind of thing.

Anyway, Lora takes it, wipes her eyes, smiles at me, and stuffs the hanky up her sleeve.

4

ELLIS WON WITH his poem in the competition last night.
I know he's proud as punch, but Mam's in no mood for
pride.

'Where did you get to last night, and what time did you get
back?' she asks. That's one trait I can't understand – Mam knows
Ellis went for a pint to celebrate, so why does she have to ask?
Mam says Ellis shouldn't go for a pint, as he's a Sunday School
teacher.

'Well, didn't I have to join the lads for a little celebration?'
he tries. 'It was a good competition, Mam. Twelve poems, good
ones at that, and guess who won first prize?'

Mam tut-tuts. Boasting's one of the deadliest sins of course,
worse even than drinking beer while being a Sunday School
teacher. Even so, Ellis gets the biggest share of the lobscouse so
Mam isn't really cross with him, I suppose.

'Come to the table before it gets cold,' Mam says sharply.

Enid puts her sewing work on top of mine in the sewing
basket, and Mam's darning slips on to the stone flags, Mam
glares at her.

'Take care, Enid. You're so clumsy sometimes.'

I give Enid's arm a little squeeze. Fair play, Enid doesn't
deserve Mam's prickly words, but then Mam's in such a strange
mood these days, blowing hot and cold, not at all like her usual
self.

Ellis is fit and well, according to the army. He had to go
up to Wrexham to the Welsh Fusiliers, so that they could tell
he's fit and well. I don't understand it, we all know he's as fit

as a fiddle – he needn't have gone all that way just for them to tell us something we all know. Ellis is never ill. Even if he goes up Ffridd Ddu without his cap on the coldest day, or sits up all night thinking up his poetry, he never gets as much as a sniffle. He's up all night these days trying to finish a long poem before he leaves. I would have caught pneumonia, but Ellis is fine. That's why I've stopped worrying about him leaving for Liverpool and the training camp – Ellis will be fine. He always comes through.

'What are you two sewing, then?' Ellis has stuffed the whole crust into his mouth all at once.

'Ellis!' Mam scowls at him, but he just smiles and pulls a face when Mam isn't looking.

He knows she's not really cross with him – she never can be properly cross with Ellis: he's the favourite, her firstborn son. She's so proud of him – we all are – but I sometimes feel for Ifan and Bob. We all know Mam has a special place in her heart for Ellis. Bob works alongside Ellis and Tada on the farm, and Bob's the best farmer – Ellis is too much of a dreamer. If the farm was left to Ellis, the sheep would be down in the village, ripping the flowers out of their beds. He leaves gaps in the hedges and gates unlatched.

I'm sent to bed with Enid, even though I'm much older than her, but Ellis has the run of the kitchen, writing his poems until dawn breaks. These past months he sits there, just thinking up elegies for his lost friends. I often wonder if any of the young men of Trawsfynydd will survive this terrible war. Then in the morning, Bob and Ifan get up to tend to the animals.

Last week, Ellis stayed up until dawn again. He's writing a poem, an *awdl*. I asked Maggie what an *awdl* is, and Maggie says it's a very long, ambiguous poem that only very clever people can understand, and it usually has something to do with the Almighty or the work of His hands. I don't think I want to read it. Anyway, he was up until dawn, then Maggie got up, cleared his papers away, and tied them neatly with string, while he went to bed.

Then sometime after nine, two strangers arrived, looking for Ellis. One was a minister and the other a scholar or poet, or something clever – they'd come to meet Ellis, and to talk about poetry. Mam ushered them into the parlour, closing the door after them, knowing that Ellis was upstairs fast asleep, but we couldn't let them know that.

'Oh yes, Ellis is at home – he's about somewhere,' Mam said. I thought it was a very clever way of putting it. She hadn't lied, after all – as lying is a sin, of course – but she didn't want to tell them he was in bed. What would they think? Ellis Evans, the poet Hedd Wyn, in bed and it being past nine.

Enid hurried upstairs to wake him, and I got his shoes to the bottom of the stairs. He came flying down, his clothes all messy, stuck his feet in the shoes and went out and round the house, so that he'd pass in front of the window so the two visitors could see him coming back, as if he'd been out in the fields. I think the visitors knew it was a trick and that Ellis had just jumped out of bed – his hair was like the fur of an angry cat and his shirt tail out of his breeches.

But Ellis is a poet, so he can get away with being a little bit odd. He has a special name, a *nom de plume* – Lora says that every poet has to have a special name. The visitors called him Hedd Wyn, but he's just Ellis to us – or, when he's being funny and fooling around, we'll sometimes call him Elsyn.

We like to tease him, calling him Hedd Wyn like they do in the eisteddfodau, and making our voices sound shaky and dramatic.

'Will Hedd Wyn come forward on to the stage and claim his prize?' And Ellis will bow and walk regally towards the table to claim Tada's chair.

'Shush, you rowdy lot in the back!' Bob will glare at us, as if he was the Master of Ceremonies. 'Can't you see that we have Hedd Wyn with us tonight?'

Once, during one of our mock ceremonies, Ellis rushed at Enid because she was making a hissing noise. Enid tried to get away, but her foot went into the milk bucket, and the whole thing tipped, emptying its contents over the stone flags. Even Ellis had a telling off that day.

'Oh, Hedd Wyn, what if Jini Owen found out about the mess you just made!'

Jini Owen was Ellis's latest sweetheart, and once Bob got hold of a poem Ellis had written for her, along with a strand of white heather.

'Oh, how sweet – listen now: *Jini, my love, always remember: my love for you is so very tender!*'

Bob had to run for his life that day, his hobnailed boots ringing out down the path, and Ellis in pursuit. I hope Jini will wait for him. I have this feeling she's the right one for Ellis, somehow.

It's the beginning of January and a freezing wind has us all in its grip. This place will be strange without Ellis, I'll miss the laughter and lightness he brings. He has time to listen, and that's important because sometimes I need to say things, work out things I don't understand. Ellis helps me work things out.

Enid's still downcast after Mam's sharp words. It wasn't really her fault that Mam's sewing ended up on the floor.

'What have you got in the sewing basket, Enid?' Ellis asks.

'Nothing.' Enid's sulking.

'It's a very pretty nothing with all those fancy stitches,' he laughs. 'Can you knit a sock yet, Enid?'

'*I* can, I can get the heel done and all!' I shout. Enid scowls at me.

'Go on then, make me a pair, Anni. I'll be needing warm

socks in that training camp. And will you make me a scarf, Enid, with that grey wool?'

'Why will you need a scarf?' Enid asks.

'That Litherland place is right on the Mersey, so they say, and the mist comes in with that cold sea, freezing rats as they scuttle.' He makes a shuffling sound and wiggles his fingers underneath the tablecloth, and we scream.

Ellis will be leaving for the army camp at the end of the month. Lora says they have to train – I'm not sure exactly what that means, but he has to train to be a soldier. I wonder if you can learn to be a soldier, because soldiers kill people. I doubt if any officer can teach Ellis to be a soldier. It took him long enough to twist the rooster's neck for our Christmas dinner, but one thing I know – killing a bird for roasting and killing a man are two different deeds entirely, even if the man's a Hun. And Ellis will be the worst soldier ever.

5

THE TRUNK'S SITTING there beneath the window, a great big shadowy beast, waiting. I hate it. Mam keeps on remembering things to put into it: warm shirts, knitted gloves, a woolly cap. I give her the knitted socks that I managed to finish, so that she can put them in. I think I did a good job of the heel bit, but Enid scowled, and said it was a mess. The trunk with its great big belly is almost full, and Ellis will be leaving in two days. Strange how the same measure of time can sometimes be so different. I want time to stop now, but it charges on, like a stupid bullock let loose after winter.

'Will you need all these papers?' Tada peers into the trunk, and clutches at the tied sheaf of loose foolscap. I can see the handwriting, blotted and untidy, words and whole sentences with black, inky lines through them. They look like crows up in the papery sky on a gloomy day, trying to form some kind of sense – but nothing makes sense these days.

'Yes, I need to take them with me. I might be able to carry on with it.' Ellis takes the bundle and puts it back in the trunk. He's almost cross with Tada. Maggie's the only one allowed to touch his papers – without Maggie's care, most of them would be scattered around the kitchen table, and his *awdl* lost.

I want to hug Tada, he looks so forlorn and sad. Ellis never raises his voice to anyone, but we all know that the skulking beast of a trunk sitting there beneath the window is unsettling each and every one of us. I agree with Tada, it would make sense to leave the foolscap and have more room for useful things. The minister's wife has sent up a basket full of groceries – sugar, tea, damson jam – and Mam's baking all day, wrapping fruit loaves in brown paper, and stuffing them into the trunk. I suspect he has plenty of warm clothes by now, but those papers won't help when he's cold and hungry, with the bitter wind from the Mersey howling through Litherland.

I'm on my way down to see Aunty Kitty. She sent some sugar up to Yr Ysgwrn the other day, but Ellis says I should take her half a dozen eggs, as her needs are greater than his, with Uncle Ifor coming home and all that. I'm yo-yoing up and down to the village on errands all day. I don't mind, as it keeps my head from running silly thoughts.

Somehow I know as soon as Aunty Kitty opens the door that something isn't right there. Aunty Kitty's one of my favourite people, and usually when I get to the door, she knows I'm there and ushers me in straight away, even if Lora isn't at home, and we sit and have a nice tittle-tattle. But today she stands in the door, not opening it, just peering out at me, and beyond the door I can hear someone moving, the slow scrape of the chair along the flagstones.

'Just a minute, Anni,' she says, the door ajar, her face strained and pale, then she closes the door and I stand there, waiting.

I can hear the door of the back bedroom opening and closing gently, then Lora appears and I follow her in out of the cold. The instant I see Lora's face, I know for sure that something is very much off-kilter. Her face is ashen, her eyes stricken and far away, and she just lets me pass her into the warm kitchen. A strange coldness takes hold of me, an iciness slithering down my throat and settling on my heart. I can't look at Lora. Then I remember my errand, and pass her the basket with the eggs. She takes it silently, carefully placing the eggs in the brown bowl on the dresser, and passing the basket back. She then takes the stool, sits down and points as if to tell me I should sit, and there we sit: huddled, clutching our knees, trying to think of something to say.

The kitchen looks the same – nothing's changed. The table's laid with the heavy red cloth, the lamp claiming centre stage, and the small window letting a sliver of the winter afternoon's grey light in through the lace curtain, the aspidistra casting long black shapes on the window ledge. I'm glad we don't have an aspidistra in our house. We don't have lace curtains either. Bob says we don't have them because spiders get stuck in the lace, and when they try and get away, they have to leave their spindly legs behind. I don't think that's why we don't have lace curtains. It's because Lora's house is right on the street, and they have a lace curtain so that prying eyes like Gwen Jones's can't look inside, and watch Jim *bach* failing to get the spoon into his mouth and the porridge getting all over his shirt front. I stare for a while at the light fading, looking for the spider legs in the lace – but I know Bob's a liar, and I don't see any.

Lora just sits, staring at nothing.

'Is Jim here?' I venture quietly.

I don't think Lora's heard – she just stares at the blue flames licking at the side of the grate. I know that blue flames are a sure sign of snow. If the snow comes, then the train might not be able to get through Cwm Prysor, and then Ellis might be allowed to stay at home until spring comes, and by then the war might be over, and we might be able to live happily ever after.

I start to silently say my prayers. *Dear Lord, please give us snow, not just a little flurry but great big drifts as high as the hedges. Please make it snow so heavily that the men from the Welsh Fusiliers can't come calling, and please make the snow go on until the war ends... Thank you, Oh Heavenly Father, and thank you for, for... for making my cough better, Amen.* I'm not sure if it was God who got rid of my cough, I think it was that stinky cloth with goose fat that Mam made me wear to bed that did the trick.

But when you ask God for something, you have to thank Him for something else – it's the way to do it, it's not as simple as just asking Him for something. It's a bit like bargaining with your little sister: *You can have the blue marble if you fetch the water once. Fetch the water four times, and you can choose the marble.* It's called bartering, but in a nice voice.

I search the room, looking for a clue, but all is exactly as it was. Then Lora looks at me and nods her head towards the darkened door of the back bedroom.

'It's Tada,' she says. 'He's come home.'

'Oh?' I swallow hard. Then our worst fears must be true. Is he like the doolally man in Blaenau, screaming and shouting in the street all night?

'What... When did he come home, Lora?'

'This morning – he came on the early train. He was here before any of us were up... before anyone could see him.'

'Have you seen him, Lora?'

'Yes.'

'Is he... is he...?' *Dear Lord in Heaven.... Oh God, please don't let Lora's tada be doolally. Dear Lord be merciful ... and I promise to learn all my verses for Sunday School. I'll even learn the whole chapter of the resurrection according to Luke, word perfect. I promise to get the water every day without being asked, and I'll give Enid my best ribbon, and my glass brooch... but please, Lord, don't let Lora's tada be doolally.'*

My eyes must have been closed, because when I look for Lora, she's standing by the front door.

'Take him for a little while again, will you?' Her other brothers have come, bringing Jim with them from their Nain's house. Lora tries to grab Jim by the arm, but he's too quick. He rushes in, past his sister, past me with my outstretched arms, and goes straight for the back bedroom. Lora screams 'No!', but Jim's in, past his mother in the doorway. I join Lora, rushing to stop him from entering the room where Uncle Ifor's hiding, but he scampers ahead of us, and that's when we hear the shriek. A shrill, terrified scream, wail upon wail, until it reaches a mad crescendo. I try to block out the sound – it reminds me of the pigs on slaughter day. I stop in the doorway, watching as Aunty Kitty gets hold of him and presses the child to her, rocking his body to and fro, murmuring comforting sounds into the curly mop, until the sobbing calms. But he still struggles to free himself and escape from the dark shadow sitting there on the edge of the bed. My mind rails – I can't make out what I'm seeing. What is that broken spectre sitting there in semi-darkness? Is it a man... a monster... an ogre? Then the sound erupts from my throat, without me even realising that it's me doing the screaming, and Lora's pulling me away.

'Come out, Anni, come out, Anni, please come away... please stop...'

She's got her arms around my waist, pulling me away, pulling me towards the open door. But it's too late, I've seen him. It's a man, a human being, with human legs, arms, shoulders and throat, but his face... I can't make out what I've seen, but it isn't the face of Uncle Ifor that I've witnessed. It's a withered face, like a wax effigy that's been left too close to an open flame, melted and deformed, red and purple scars writhing through the greying flesh, and the mouth... there was no mouth, just an empty, gaping, cavity.

'Hello!' a voice from the open front door shakes me back into reality. 'Hello, it's just me...'

A warm, familiar face looks in on us – it's Ellis. I stand there transfixed: someone's beaten invisible nails through the soles of my shoes and I'm stuck fast to the floorboards. I just look at Ellis, and the smile on his face fades.

'What is it, Anni?' He comes forward into the room, and Aunty Kitty comes towards us, Jim clinging to her, still sobbing.

'Mam, no, no!' he's shouting, and starts to kick again, struggling to get away from the broken man in the back bedroom. Aunty Kitty puts him down and I listen as his scrambling footsteps fade down the street.

'Leave him, Lora,' she says, as Lora starts to go after him. 'He'll go to Nain's. Ellis, come in.'

'How are you Kit? I heard Ifor was back...' says Ellis.

'Yes, he came this morning. We are as you see us, Ellis *bach*.' Aunty Kitty sits heavily on the stool, reaching out to the flames for comfort. She looks towards the closed door of the back bedroom.

'He's in a bad way, Ellis. I don't know if you should see him, it's his face... but... I must be strong. I have him at home, and he will get better.'

Ellis and Uncle Ifor are good friends, but somehow I don't want Ellis to go in.

'No!' Everyone turns to look at me.

'I should see him, Kit, if he agrees.'

'No!' I shout. 'We must go home, Ellis. Mam will be waiting for us, with you going away and all that.'

'Anni!' I know that Ellis is cross with me. 'Don't be silly,' he says. 'We'll go, but let me just put my head in to say hello first.'

He glares at me, but he doesn't know what I know. He stands there with his cap in his hands, waiting for the go-ahead from Aunty Kitty. Shortly she comes back out of the back bedroom, leaving the door ajar, so that Ellis can pass her.

'He wants to see you, Ellis,' she nods.

'No!' I whisper. I don't want Ellis to see what I've seen. It's the war that's done this to Uncle Ifor, the war that Ellis is going to join in just two days. I turn away from him, clutching at Lora, and we both stand there, holding tight, sobbing.

6

H ow does Wil Ferret always seem to turn up when you least want to see his sneaky face?

'Where are you off to?'

He pokes his rat-like snout at us, sniffing out any crumb of gossip, then he follows us as we struggle back uphill. We've just been to Lora's grandmother's.

We had to leave Jim there with his gran, with Nain. He was curled up in the chair, his arms over his head, still terrified, the strangeness of it all haunting him. I know how he feels, and I wish we didn't have to go back to Lora's house, but Nain says we must.

'You leave Jim here with me, Lora *fach*. He'll come round, you'll see. Go home – your mother needs all the help she can get now. Lord only knows what will become of you...'

The old woman bent over Jim and gently stroked his light curls until we could hear his breath easing. I know that Lora would rather have stayed there all curled up in the chair by the hearth too, with Nain gently brushing her curls out of her face, but when you're 14, you're expected to get up and find something useful to do – something useful like throwing stones at Wil Ferret.

'So, your Dad's really home then, Lora?'

Lora doesn't stop. I pause. Should I say something? I decide to keep my mouth shut, and follow Lora up the road towards her house, and the strangeness.

'He came on the early train, I heard?' Wil tries.

Lora and I link arms and flee up the hill towards Lora's house,

Wil following at a safe distance. He knows from experience that I'm the best shot at shin target. I might just ask my brother Ifan to come down to the village and warn Wil off. But then again, that's no way to do it. I must stand up for myself.

'Is he home on leave, then, Lora?' Wil persists. He only wants to know so that he can go around the village with that air of his – he just wants to *know* things. The schoolmaster always tells us that '*The ears of the wise seek out knowledge*', but I don't think that's the same thing as knowing the latest gossip. Wil's ears stick out and they're anything but wise.

'Well, is it leave he's got, Lora?' He doesn't really care why Uncle Ifor is home.

Once Ned – Lora's brother – got the cane at school for getting 'Gallipoli' wrong in his spelling test. Wil saw Lora's mother on his way home from school that day and just had to blurt out about the caning. Ned almost got another stroke of the cane from Aunty Kitty, until she realised that his only crime was having misspelt the name of a place almost no one had heard of, and then she just gave poor Ned a bigger share of the loaf.

Wil Ferret is just a little rat, a *snichyn*.

Then I realise that Wil's got company. There's another lad lurking at the bottom of the hill. I peer, but can't make out his face. He comes a little closer, scuffing at the loose gravel on the side of the road as he does. He's a little older than us, perhaps 15 or 16, and his dark hair casts a shadow over his face. He nears slowly, as if he's reluctant to be part of Wil's questioning.

'Is your father glad to be home, Lora?' Wil's gaze is still on Lora, but she keeps her eyes averted, and doesn't say a word.

'Is he in the house?' Not a word.

'Has he got his uniform on?' Not a word.

It's then that he realises that we've stopped and have noticed the boy nearing the top of the hill, coming towards us.

'I know who he is.' At last, he's got our full attention. He stops, waiting – waiting for us to ask. But we know that he wants us to ask, so we turn again as if to head for Lora's door – we'll let the *snichyn* squirm.

'Well?'

'Well, what?'

'Well, do you want me to tell you who he is?'

But by this time the stranger has reached the top of Lora's street. Wil's chance of sharing any information is almost lost, and that can't be allowed to happen, so he blurts:

'He's come to stay with his aunt, as he's starting as a farmhand near Frongoch next week.' Then he mumbles something, as he realises that the lad has come up and is standing just behind him. I almost feel sorry for Wil then.

Lora holds on to my arm, and the lad looks at us shyly.

'Are you Ifan and Bob's sister?' he asks. I nod, dumbly. I can feel my cheeks burning. Damn stupid cheeks. Why must my face burn like that, here in front of Wil and this strange lad? It's because of rushing uphill of course. Has the lad noticed? Then he turns his dark eyes to look at Lora.

'I'm sorry,' he says. 'I'm afraid I don't know you.'

'Lora!' shouts Wil. 'She's Lora Margaret, and she lives right there, and her father has just come home, and...'

We both stare at the strange lad, who stands there awkwardly at the edge of the street. Wil's jumped up on to the wall, his darting eyes watching. I think Wil should go into writing newspaper stories – nothing gets by him.

'Lora Margaret and...' the stranger's eyes move towards me.

'Anni.' I barely whisper my name.

'She lives up at Yr Ysgwrn, and she has another older brother. He writes poems and things, but even he has to go away to war now, you see – even poets have to,' Wil persists. 'And this lad's name is Huw – see girls, I know.'

'I'm so pleased to meet you both,' Huw chuckles, amused by

the show. He gives a little bow and touches his cap, as if he's greeting two ladies. I like him. Lora clutches at my hand. We both know that there's something different about this young man – he's a gentleman, and there's mystery lurking in those dark eyes.

Then he glances up at Wil, perched up on the wall.

'Huw Arthur Williams. That's my full name, so that you know.'

Wil scowls, picking at the lichen on the stone wall.

'And I've come to stay with my aunt in the village, I'm not sure if Wil mentioned that.'

Lora just gapes at him, her mouth open, fishlike. I poke her in the ribs. She turns to protest, but I tug at her arm – she knows as well as I do that ladies don't gawk at people like that, especially at young men. As we turn back towards Lora's house, Huw calls after us.

'Good evening, ladies! Will I see you at the Band o'Hope tomorrow evening?'

'Of course!' I stop and call, but Lora doesn't say a word.

I feel a sudden warm rush flowing through my veins. Is it because of Huw? Or perhaps it's Lora's grip, as she's still clutching at me.

'I'll come with you, Anni, to the Band o'Hope, if Mam agrees. Will you call for me?' We've almost reached the house. 'Will you call, Anni?'

'Yes, Lora, I'll call for you.'

Then it comes back to me: the nagging whine in my ear. What right do I have to feel excited, to look forward to the Band o'Hope? I shouldn't be happy, should I? Not with all the sadness surrounding me, all the worry.

Ellis appears on his way out – he's been in with Uncle Ifor all this time. Aunty Kitty follows him out into the street, and I can see the strain on her face. Ellis nods, standing there, turning his cap round and round in his hands as he does whenever he's uneasy. He's saying something, comforting words, then he pats her arm, and Aunty Kitty gets her hanky out of her sleeve. Then he turns and sees us there, and I know that something's changed in Ellis as he leaves that house. The house where in the long shadows his friend Ifor sits, hiding from prying eyes beyond the bedroom door.

'Come on, Anni, we'd better get home.'

I struggle to catch him up. He strides ahead, his body bent against the cold wind, his cap over his eyes.

'Ellis...' I call, my breath caught by the bitter wind.

I want Ellis to wait. I need to ask him how it is that I want to look forward to the Band o'Hope: is it a sin? Is it a sin that I feel a lightness in me, while Aunty Kitty and Lora are thrown into such a storm?

I try to word my thoughts.

'Ellis, when your best friend is sad, is it a sin for you to feel happiness at all, you know... like Lora and me..?'

I don't think Ellis understands what I'm trying to form into a question, because he just strides on, without an answer. We walk on side by side for a while, and I glance up at his face. It has none of its usual lightness and he stares ahead, the worry darkening his face. I don't like the silence between us – it's not as it should be. I always enjoy walking home with Ellis, enjoy his banter and quips, but there's none today. We've left the village and are making our way up towards Yr Ysgwrn, the dusk drawing in, forming grey figures along the hedges, closing in on our thoughts. Then, as we reach the stile, Ellis stops suddenly.

'Anni,' he peers at me in the darkness. 'Anni, don't let this bloody war break you. You're young, you have spirit in you – don't let the sadness get through to your soul, it'll just choke you. Promise me, Anni?'

I don't know what to say. These are not usual words, they frighten me. This isn't our usual Ellis.

'We'll come through this, Anni – Ifor will get better, and the scars will fade with time. We'll get Mam to make some of her pennywort ointment, and you must take it down to Kit.'

He smiles weakly, seeing my stricken face, but it isn't a proper smile – his eyes are brimming with worry. He pauses, and looks towards the narrow strip of light that slants in through the pass between the mountains, the Rhinogydd. Beyond their giant, solid shapes lies the sea and lightness.

'Happiness is never a sin. Don't ever change, Anni – don't let this war change you.'

7

B Y THE TIME we get home, Maggie's just returned by the last train from her trip to Liverpool, and everyone's huddled beside the fire listening to her account of all the fabulous things she's seen in the city. She tries to walk gracefully, mimicking the ladies, an imaginary wide-brimmed hat perched precariously on her head – while trying to avoid the chairs, Ifan's legs and numerous other obstacles in the small kitchen.

'And Mam, their shoes – you'd love a pair! Made with the softest leather, and the heel so narrow, and the ladies all balancing on them, and they had a little shiny buckle on the side. So elegant, they were – and their short skirts, showing their ankles. And the motor cars, Ifan...'

'Ladies showing their ankles?' tut-tuts Mam. 'No one should show their ankles, and to think that in Liverpool they show their ankles on the street!'

'Did you get to ride in a motor car, Maggie?' Ifan asks, trying to make room for his long legs underneath the table. I love it when everyone's at home, everyone together in the kitchen, close and warm.

'No, Ifan, only the fine families get to ride in the motor cars. Still, shops are beginning to use motor vans to take their groceries from door to door... By the time the war is over, we'll have motor cars in Trawsfynydd – you'll see.'

'Huh! You stick with those long legs of yours, Ifan, or a bicycle. I'll have no motor cars here. Tricky things, motor cars – those engines could blow you to smithereens in a jiffy.'

But Ifan just scowls at Tada. I think Ifan will have a motor car one day, and perhaps he'll take me to Barmouth to the seaside in it.

I think Ifan's a little jealous of Ellis. He'd love a trip to Liverpool, because engines and machines are just what he likes. When the landlord and his gentlemen friends come here on their hunting trips, Ifan will hang around all day, gawping at their motor cars, going round and round, trying to figure out how the engine does this, what makes that work, what if... Oh, he'd just love it.

Maggie turns to Ellis.

'I went to a show one evening, Ellis – it was a kind of a magic lantern show, except that they called it *the pictures*. It explained why the soldiers have to go and fight, you see. The pictures showed Belgium as a beautiful, lonely young lady stranded on a long bare beach, and then this nasty-looking bird of prey with the Kaiser's face swooped down towards her, picked her up in its talons and took her to his nest somewhere in Germany...'

Maggie pauses and pretends to swoop at Enid, like the nasty Kaiser bird, and Enid squeals and chuckles.

'Then British troops appeared and tried to save the Belgian beauty, and then everyone watching started to cheer and sing. And the soldiers who were watching – most of them from Litherland, Ellis, and they were in their uniforms, so we knew who they were – well, they were hoisted on to shoulders and carried out into the street, everyone cheering them on. It was a proper circus. And I met Islwyn Francis, you know – he's from Blaenau isn't he? He was there, and he told me to tell you that he'll be at Litherland, and that he'll look out for you. He says that the camp is fine, not bad at all; so Mam, we're not to worry, he said.'

Maggie's pulling things out of her bag – a coloured card for

Enid, with a pretty young lady dressed in a white gown and flowers in her hair painted on it. Then it's my turn – a piece of red satin ribbon.

For a moment the excitement of Maggie's return blanks out our worry and paints over our feelings, but I know that it'll take just a scratch in the flaky veneer of happiness and we'll all see the darkness beneath once again. And it's just so. Just a glimpse of Ellis, who hasn't even taken his overcoat off and is just sitting there, crumpled, looking into the flames. Maggie looks from Ellis to me. I try to smile, but it's just a crooked grimace. She looks at Mam, and Mam shrugs her shoulders.

The laughter and excitement is spent, like a flame under a glass jar. The wonders of Liverpool are gone. If Ellis is downcast, then everyone else is downcast – that's how we are.

The supper eaten and dishes cleared, Enid and I are sent to bed. It's unfair – she's so much younger than I am, I should be able to stay up later – but tonight's not the time to argue my case. I have to accompany her: sometimes she's such a cry baby. She insists that something hides in the shadows at the top of the landing and blows out the candle once she gets to the last step. But I know it's because she opens the bedroom door too quickly and it's only the draught that makes the flame flicker and go out. I suppose it doesn't help that I once played a trick on her and balanced Mam's fur on top of the door, so that it dropped and brushed her face when she pushed the half-open door. That time she screamed so loudly that I was afraid she'd have a convulsion fit and kick the bucket there and then – I almost died of fright myself. I was so shaken that even Mam couldn't bring herself to tell me off.

On my way to bed, I place my shoe gently against the kitchen door, so that it doesn't shut tightly – that way I can creep back down to sit on the bottom step on the stairs and listen to their conversation. I know that that's when the truth gets told – when Enid and I are in bed.

Enid tucks herself up beside me.

'Do you like the picture Maggie gave me?' she asks, yawning. I know how to get Enid to sleep – I just have to be very nice to her. 'Of course,' I say. 'One day we'll have white gowns, just the same as the lady in the picture, and I'll tie flowers in your hair, and you'll look like an angel flown down directly from God Himself. And everyone will say, *Oh, look at Enid, isn't she just beautiful?* And you can borrow my red ribbon to tie on your dress next Sunday for Sunday School, if you like.' I stroke her curls gently in a monotonous motion.

There. She's asleep.

Silently, I slip out of bed, the oilcloth covering the floorboards on the landing freezing beneath my feet. I pull on my socks and drape my coat over my nightie. I know one of the floorboards is loose, so I step over it, grasping the banister. I take my seat on the lowest step, and listen. Through the narrow gap between door and frame, the light of the fire dances, creating mystical shapes along the wooden partition, twisted fingers jumping towards me. At first everyone just sits there, watching the flames, all deep in their own thoughts. Then Tada speaks, his voice low and tight.

'Will Ifor have to go back to the trenches, Ellis?

'No, I doubt it. He's very broken, Tada – I don't know how Kit'll be able to persuade him to leave the back bedroom.'

'Will he work again?'

'I don't know who'll take him on, Tada – it's his face.'

'Was it gas?'

'No.' I have to strain to hear my brother's words. It's as if some unseen force is moving, dragging the words from him. 'No, it was a shell blast to his jaw. It was a miracle that he lived.'

'Good Lord!'

I sit there shivering, the ticking of the clock filling the silence. Then Ellis gets up and stands there in front of the hearth, poking the fire.

'He's lost half his face, Tada – his chin is gone. They had to rebuild his face, bit by bit, like shaping a piece of clay. His mouth's just a black void, his words just a gargling sound – he'll need all the care Kit can give...' Then Ellis turned to Tada, 'I don't know if I can be brave like that. I don't know how all this will end.'

Mam gets up and clutches his arm.

'We'll have to be brave,' she gasps, 'like Kitty.'

Ellis nods.

'Yes, like Kit. They'll get through, but I don't know how Jim *bach* will come to terms with it. He can do nothing but scream whenever he claps eyes on Ifor.'

'It's too early yet for the little one. I'll go down tomorrow, and Anni will come with me,' says Mam.

'Perhaps we could take Ifor on here as a hand for a while, just until he gets sorted... We'll need all the help we can get, what with you leaving, Ellis.' Tada gets up: it's late. I hurry back up the stairs and slip silently under the eiderdown beside Enid. Soon Tada and Mam are speaking in hushed, sober, voices behind the adjoining partitioning. Maggie comes quietly into the bedroom and gets into her bed beneath the window. I keep silent, pretending to be asleep. Bob and Ifan are in bed, but I know Ellis is still sitting there in the darkened kitchen.

I lie there for a while watching the light of the moon on the ceiling, following the cracks in the whitewash. Tada and Mam are silent now, and Maggie's steady breathing reveals that sleep has overcome her. I slither out of bed, pull on my socks and coat once again, and make my way back down the stairs, forgetting about the creaking step. It makes a loud cracking sound. I jump, but no one from upstairs stirs, though Ellis doesn't seem surprised to see me when I open the kitchen door. He's sitting in the circle of lamplight by the table, his papers a messy heap.

'Could you not get to sleep, Anni?' he asks.

'No,' I whisper, settling down by the fire.

'Why?'

'I can't stop thinking, Ellis.'

'Thinking is good, Anni.' His voice is sober. 'Not when you should be asleep perhaps, but don't stop thinking things through. This whole mess is as it is because powerful men didn't do enough thinking.'

I steal a glance at the pile of papers on the table.

'What are you doing, Ellis?' He was away in the midst of his poem, his special words. I can't see how he'll be able to carry on with them in Litherland.

'I'm working on the *awdl*, Anni, the one that needs to be sent to the National Eisteddfod at Birkenhead. I should finish it before I go, but I doubt that I'll be able to, what with everything else that needs doing.'

I don't think he'll be able to work on poems when he has to get the killing training done.

'What's the poem about, Ellis?' I don't usually ask him about his poems, but perhaps I should know about this one. 'Is it a happy poem?'

'It's an ode – a long poem – and it... well, its title's "The Hero".' He gives me a quizzical look. I'm not expected to understand, but I need in some way to fathom his thoughts, decipher his words. He stares at the paper in front of him, and I keep quiet and still. After a while he looks up and smiles at me.

'Perhaps not a happy poem, Anni, not in the way you mean; but I intend it to be inspiring in a way. Do you remember when you asked me earlier if you had the right to be happy when there was so much sadness and suffering surrounding you?'

I nod, and wait for him to continue.

'Well, I'm trying to reassure us all that good will prevail, that all this sadness and misery will come to an end, because there is more good in the world than bad. And in a strange way this goodness is the 'hero'... because it strives to rise above all evil. And when people strive to end evil and to reach out for fairness and dignity for all, then the world will be a contented place.'

He pushes back his chair and reaches for my hand.

'Come on, Anni, put on your shoes. The moon's shining, come on.'

We go out into the small yard and look away towards the mountains; a cluster of squatting giants, grey and solid by the light of the moon.

'Look up, Anni!' Ellis says. 'Look at all the stars, the mystery of them, their number – it's unfathomable. Look at the brightness of them. Nothing can smother that brightness, except of course the light of dawn, and when dawn comes then everything seems better. When I'm away in Litherland, and if I have to go on to the trenches, Anni, I want you to look at the stars and remember what I told you tonight. No one can snuff out the stars. Nothing can smother the brightness that's in you: don't let that happen.'

We go back into the kitchen and Ellis puts some milk to warm by the fire. Warm milk's good for helping you to get to sleep. We drink our milk silently, and I go back to bed. I pull back the curtain so that I can see the stars as I lie there in bed, but I must fall straight to sleep because I don't see any.

8

'DO YOU THINK he'll be there?' asks Lora. I've just called for her, and we're on our way to the Band o'Hope.

I went down to her house yesterday with Mam, taking pennywort ointment with us. The ointment might help with the fading of the scars, but it can do nothing to heal the missing part of Uncle Ifor's chin.

I always knock now when I go to Lora's house. It's strange having to knock, but Uncle Ifor doesn't want anyone to see him yet, and he has to have a forewarning that we're coming so he can go into the back bedroom, out of sight. Lora says he has a leather mask to wear, but it's stuffy and uncomfortable.

'Do you think Huw will turn up?' Lora asks. We get to the chapel early, and sit down on the bench in the chapel vestry with the other girls. All the girls sit on one side of the aisle, and the boys on the opposite side. There's the usual riot going on, the banter and *hwyl* almost getting out of hand. Someone's got hold of Wil Ferret's cap and is throwing it along the aisle. Deio Mawr's got it now, and as he's a giant of a lad, Wil has to jump up to try and retrieve it from Deio's hands. I almost feel sorry for Wil, but I change my mind immediately when Wil shouts out for everyone to hear that I'm wearing my red ribbon in my hair because Huw's expected at the Band o'Hope. My face is almost as red as the flaming ribbon. One day I'll get hold of Wil, the little rat, and his head will be in the ditch. I could do it – he's only a wretched little weasel.

Mr Jones has just got up, and the noise gradually dies down He reminds us again about our temperance promise: all of us at the Band o'Hope have made a pledge not to let a 'drop of Satan's water pass our lips, and to keep on the straight and narrow road that will take us up towards the light that is our Lord Almighty...'

His words trail off as he turns to point to the painting that hangs above him on the vestry wall. I know this painting like I know the lines on my own hand. To one side of the painting there's a shining white cloud which radiates light, and in the centre a kind face appears. This must be God – I always puzzle how the artist knows what God's face looks like. And if God's such a nice, kind being, why does He let Ellis go to war, and furthermore, why did He send Uncle Ifor home with half his face missing? *God works in mysterious ways* is the only answer I have to my questions. I try to force these thoughts out of my mind – Mr Jones says they're blasphemous, and blasphemy's a sin. I concentrate on the painting. A few diminutive figures in tidy, clean clothes walk up the narrow path towards the face in the white cloud. There's a sunny kind of aurora radiating from them and on all sides of the narrow path there are chapels and churches. Everything's orderly and proper.

Then on the other side of the painting there's a matching cloud, except that this one's dark and stormy looking, and from its depths an evil red face leers. A wide path snakes towards the cloud, and along it throng wretched-looking figures, their clothes ragged and dirty. Women in short skirts with their ankles showing hang on to their scruffy-looking husbands, and barrels of beer, spirit bottles and tankards are discarded along the way.

Mr Jones continues to rail against the *demon drink* and its consequences, but no one is listening so his voice rises in competition with the rowdiness. His voice resonates around the bare chapel walls and reaches an almost hysterical pitch, until all I can decipher are the words *Hell's fire, Hell's fire, Hell's fire.*

At that moment, sitting on a hard bench, feet and hands

frozen, breath rising white and clammy, no one seems affected by the threat of fire – Hell's or otherwise.

I wonder if the ladies Maggie saw in Liverpool are similar to those in the painting? Then I get a poke from Lora and a stirring rushes through the benches, especially the benches where the girls are sitting. We all gawp, necks twisted towards the open door at the back of the chapel, where the dark-haired lad's standing.

Mr Jones has to wave the *sol-fa* stick, threatening the boys with a bashing, before a shaky order is imposed again.

'He's here!' whispers Lora, and everyone stares as Huw comes forward, looking for a suitable space on the benches.

'I'm sorry to interrupt,' he says quietly, taking a seat near the back, as if he needs an escape route.

Somehow that evening the proceedings are even more shambolic than usual. The *sol-fa* exercise screeches on, with the boys droning every note repeatedly, until Mr Jones's face resembles the face on the dark side of the painting, and his eyes start to blink uncontrollably, which is a sure sign that an eruption's imminent. The blessing is said as soon as possible, heralding the end of the meeting, and everyone flees out into the cold, leaving Mr Jones to sink into the peace of the *sêt fawr*, the front bench reserved for those in authority at the chapel.

Everyone crowds around Huw, but we stand shyly to one side. Eventually everyone turns for home, and Huw joins us as we leave the chapel and head towards Lora's house. I'm always told to wait for Ifan, so he can accompany me up the track towards Yr Ysgwrn. But Ifan's nowhere to be seen. He's probably found his sweetheart – he doesn't come to the Band o'Hope these days. That means I'll have to wait for him later, at the end of the street.

The three of us walk on in silence, no one really knowing what to say.

'Do you like it in Frongoch?' I ask, because the growing silence is awkward.

'I haven't started my job there yet. My aunt says I should wait until this cold spell passes,' Huw replies.

'Do you like it here in Trawsfynydd, then?' I venture.

'I'm very comfortable, thank you,' he replies quietly. 'My aunt's kind, but I'd like to go home at some point.'

'Oh?' I don't know what else to say, and Lora's no help, just scuffing her shoes and dragging along.

'Home?'

'Yes, back to Harlech.'

'Is that where your parents are?' I know I'm being too forward, and if Mam knew then I'd be told off.

'Yes, my home's in Harlech, but only my mother and younger brother are there now.'

I know when to stop my questioning, so we carry on walking silently apart from the sound of our feet on the rough pavement, our breath rising into the cold air. But I can't bear the silence.

'Did you always dream of becoming a farmhand?' I ask.

'I don't mind being a farmhand. I have to do something to help, and I suppose a farmhand's as good as anything. Mam can't keep me at school.' He shrugs, but doesn't look up.

'Where's your father, then?' It's Lora – she just blurts it out. I don't know what comes over her sometimes. But Huw stops, and I can barely hear his next words.

'He's still over in France somewhere.'

'In France?' Lora stands and looks at him. 'Tada's just come home from France!' she says.

'Has he? From the Somme?' Huw looks at Lora, but I can't make out the look on his face. His eyes are bright, but his voice holds no trace of warmth. 'He's a very lucky man, then, isn't he?' he added.

'I'm not sure,' Lora mutters. I can sense the tremor in her

voice. 'I suppose so, at least we're lucky to have him at home with us.'

Huw looks perplexed but he doesn't reply. Should I say something? Give an explanation perhaps? I struggle to find the words.

'Uncle Ifor, Lora's father, he's – well, he's hurt, you see.' I remember Ellis's words: 'He's broken, somehow.'

Huw nods, a sad recognition. He pulls his cap further over his eyes, and burrows his hands deeper into his pockets. He turns as if to walk away, but then turns to Lora.

'I'm sorry about your father,' he says. 'I'd like to know, you see – I'd like to know where my father is. That's the worst of it, not knowing. No telegram came, no letter from a hospital, no sign, no one can tell us anything. We have nothing, we know nothing of him – nothing.'

We don't know how to reply, so we just stand there staring at the poor boy.

'All we know is that on that morning in Mametz, he crossed the wire out of the trench with his company... and that's it. Six months have passed, and we've heard nothing of him.'

Ifan never appears when I need him. Why doesn't he just saunter around the street corner, calling for me to hurry up, saying it's time to get along home. But he's nowhere to be seen. It's Lora's nain who comes to break the silence. She's got Jim by the hand, but I can tell she's struggling to get him to follow her.

'Lora, please come and take your brother,' she calls. Is Jim going to have one of his screaming fits there in the middle of the street?

Huw's reached the end of the street, and Lora rushes to help Nain. She takes the child in her arms, whispering reassuring words, stroking his cheek, turning up his coat collar against that bitter wind.

'Your mother wants him home Lora,' says Nain. 'I tried to

tell her that she should leave him with me for a day or two, until he gets used to things, you know, but she'll have none of it. So home it is, *bach*.'

Lora clutches Jim tightly against her chest, and the child rests his cheek on her shoulder.

'He'll be fine with me, Nain. We'll get by, right as rain – you'll see.' But the old woman just shakes her head and mutters her protests as she goes back downhill towards her own home.

Lora puts Jim down and we each take one of his hands. Only Aunty Kitty's there in the kitchen when we get in. She smiles and takes Jim in her arms. Sitting in the rocking chair and holding the child tightly, he's soon asleep.

'Where did you two get to?' she asks.

'We walked home with a lad called Huw who's come to stay with his aunt in the village.'

'Oh?'

'He's called Huw Arthur Williams, and he's from Harlech,' says Lora.

'Ah yes, I heard that he'd come to stay with his aunt,' says Aunty Kitty, 'Poor souls.'

I suddenly notice a shadow moving just behind the door to the back bedroom. I can hear Uncle Ifor moving. Has he been listening?

'His father was at the Somme, you know, Mam – at Mametz, like Tada – but they haven't heard a word of him since...'

The back bedroom door shuts quickly. Aunty Kitty looks up suddenly.

'Your father needs to rest, Lora, and here we are making all this noise.' But she smiles at me. I bid them all good night and prepare to walk all the way home by myself.

9

ELLIS'S KIT HAS gone ahead of him. Bob and Ifan hoisted it between them, and took it on to the station. The space where the trunk stood beneath the window is gaping and empty. In the kitchen, Maggie's fussing over the food parcel for the journey to Litherland. She ties the string, tightening the brown paper, tying and untying, but I know she's just doing it to keep her hands busy. She, like the rest of us, wants to tug at Ellis's coat-tails, to stop him from leaving. Mam holds Ellis close – it's strange, seeing her holding him like that, she looks so small – but Tada stays in his seat by the fire. Then it's Enid's and my turn. Ellis hugs us, and the rough cloth of his overcoat's coarse against my cheek.

'Be good,' he says. 'Keep at it with your knitting, Enid, and send the scarf on when it's finished.' Then he turns to face me. 'Don't forget the stars, Anni,' he says, tapping the side of his nose. It's just our secret. 'Don't forget what I told you.'

Then he turns and Tada struggles out of his chair. He reaches out his bony hand, and Ellis takes hold of it, and they both stand there for a while. I think Tada wants to reach out with both arms to hug his eldest son too, but he doesn't.

'Don't give up on the poem.' Tada tries so hard to keep his voice light. 'We could do with a new chair here, Ellis!' But no one laughs: we know there'll be one empty place around the table now with Ellis gone. Tada can't say another word.

Ellis won't allow any of us to walk with him to the station, though Bob and Ifan, of course, have already gone on ahead of him. So everyone just stands there in the passageway, but I rush upstairs, and watch as he disappears from view.

'Do you think he'll have time to write to us, Anni?' Enid's still hiccupping, tears making her voice all tight and strained.

'Of course he will, he won't be training all the time. He'll have his evenings, you see – he'll write.'

'But will he remember about my birthday, Anni? He promised me a poem for my birthday, and my birthday's next week. Do you think he'll remember?'

I glance at her, her face just a pool of tears. I hug her to me. I know what she means. I've got my birthday poem on a piece of notebook cover in my drawer – it's one of my most treasured possessions. And I know that Jini had a birthday poem written for her last summer – we know because Bob found it in Ellis's pocket and read it out to us, to Ellis's embarrassment. Today's 29 January, only four days until Enid's birthday. Will Ellis remember, or will he be too busy, what with everything else he's got on his mind?

'Come on, Enid,' I drag her downstairs. 'We'll go down to see Lora. And I'll have something special for your birthday this year, you'll see.'

I haven't even thought of her birthday yet, but I had to think of something to say that will shift her mind from the sight of Ellis's back disappearing down the path. That's me done again – always putting my foot in it, saying things without thinking them through properly. Perhaps if I ask Maggie, she'll help me make a lace flower or the like for Enid's birthday.

'Yes, let's go down to see Lora. We can help by taking Jim out for a while,' I say.

The kitchen's empty. Tada's gone out to the horses – I can hear his low voice, calming the old mare. Ellis has a way with the horses. It's not just us who'll miss him around the place.

Mam comes back with a jar of the ointment and a slab of butter, and puts them in the basket.

'Here – take these with you. Tell Kitty that I'm asking after them, and that I'll be down soon.'

I can see that the mulling's over. Mam sits heavily, reaches out for her clogs and puts them on. Jobs have to be done, and with Ellis gone, there'll be so much more work for us all now.

'Don't be long now, will you? And don't dally, the chicken coop needs cleaning out,' she says and is gone, out to the yard.

Cleaning the chicken coop out is the worst job in the world. The chicken fleas get into my hair, the smell makes me retch, and I don't like the hens either – their beady little eyes following me as I move. They're vicious, cruel creatures, their beaks ready to poke at me. One time a crow with a broken wing got stuck in the little run where the hens were scratching. A strange bird in amongst them, they pecked and clawed. It wasn't long before there was nothing of the crow, just a bloody corpse. I shudder. I don't like crows either, but I feel a sorrow for the one that got stuck in the chicken coop. Nothing deserves to die that way.

When we get down to the village, Jim's sitting on the step outside the front door, playing with the coal shovel. When he sees us approaching, he runs indoors shouting incomprehensible words – only Lora and Aunty Kitty understand his strange little sounds. Lora comes out of the back bedroom then, and I notice the tray in her hands. On it stand a white bowl, a spoon and a metal tube. I must be staring, because Lora just says, 'He's getting better. He doesn't use the tube so much now.'

I help her clear the dishes, and Enid stays outside playing with Jim, building imaginary ramparts with the gravel.

From the back bedroom I can hear Aunty Kitty's low, careful words. Sometimes I can hear Uncle Ifor's voice, but I can't make out what he's saying. Aunty Kitty's got a special gift, it seems – she can decipher words that no one else can understand.

'Has your father said anything about the battle, Lora, and what happened?' I haven't even thought of asking such a question till now, but somehow with Ellis gone, I need to know.

'He can't say anything much, you know, Anni. He just shakes his head – his tongue doesn't seem to be able to form any words.' Lora pauses, but I keep quiet and she continues, 'But I found this, look...'

She pulls out a sheaf of paper from her apron pocket. We both leave the dishes and climb the narrow stairs. She looks at the papers, as if questioning her intention to give me the bundle. Then she hands it to me. I can see they're pages torn out of an old notebook and the pages are filled with a shaky hand.

'Don't tell anyone, Anni – don't tell anyone about it.'

I start to read. I stop, and stare at Lora.

'I think he wanted to explain to Mam about the way things happened. He can't talk, can he, and there were things she needed to know. Mam had put it in the Bible, and that's where I found it.'

10

My Dear Kit,

It was 10 July - how could I forget that date? It was our day, Kit: the date that you became my wife, 18 years ago. But dear Lord, what a contrast. How can two days be so different?

We were on the edge of some woodland, a place by the name of Mametz, and we'd been preparing for the push for days. A gang of our boys making the best of pushing at the enemy line... going over the wire... but having to fall back - the gas coming at us like the rancid breath of a vicious beast, and the guns cutting us down. We were so tired, Kit, our feet long soaked in our sodden boots, skin blistering and raw, and the fleas incessantly gnawing at us. We were just rotting skin and sores.

Two brothers joined us. Do you remember the Park Place brothers, Kit? Tommy the eldest, and Ted bach. And Owen Wills, of course. We were always together, Owen and I - partners, watching out for each other. The two of us would spend hours talking about our families, you and the children, Kit, and it was as if I'd come to know his family just by listening to Owen. He had a son, a scholar... Owen had such high hopes for his son, hoping that he could carry on with his education.

Anyway, I was going to tell you about Tommy and Ted bach... Tommy was to go on an earlier mission you see, and he was worried about his young brother Ted, so he asked

Owen and myself to look out for him. Of course, he didn't have to ask - we'd always look out for each other, but Ted was so young. Tommy knew, you see, Kit. He knew, like the rest. They all knew that they wouldn't be returning. And they were right. Tommy went over the wire with the first lot, and was hit in the back - a shell - and that was that.

Ted's only 17, only a couple of years older than our Lora, Kit. He'd enlisted with the notion that he'd see a little of this great world. Ha! He changed his mind soon enough. The world didn't look that great from where we were, there at the bottom of a trench, clothes soaked, feet sore, and the rats scampering over him at night. That's how it is there, Kit, with the young lads. They enlist because they see it as an adventure. They want to prove that they're men; they want their sweethearts to be proud of them. Poor, foolish lads, they're not to know that they're heading for the blackest, foulest hell-hole on earth. It would be so much more sensible if they accepted the white feather and stayed at home.

We'd smoked the last of our tobacco by dawn, Owen and me, and we'd written our letters home... Did you receive that letter, I wonder? We were waiting, you see, Kit, waiting for the sign that it was time to go. Owen was telling Ted and me stories - fishing stories, hunting tales, anything to keep our minds away from the inevitable.

Dawn broke, and the shout came. Men started over the fence: scrambling, tripping, clambering. 'Walk,' they shouted, 'walk.' And we walked, straight into that gaping void of gunshots and screams. Our mission was to cross a bare sweep of land - there was no shelter, nothing to defend us. We needed to reach the woods at the other end, where the enemy line was, and they had the woods to hide

61

in. It was madness, Kit. All those officers... We were no experts, but any fool could see that we had no chance. We were helpless, defenceless, just walking targets.

Of course, our boys had tried to prepare the field, bombarding, firing shells, but all that had done was turn the field into deep craters and holes. And then we had Ted to look out for. When the sign came at first to go over the wire, he wouldn't move. He was frozen with fear, his hands covering his ears, cowering at the bottom of the ditch, crying like a small child. It struck me, Kit, that he was just that - a child. But I've seen men cry, strong, strapping big men, wailing. Tears are not a sign of weakness, Kit, they're just a sign that you're still human, still able to feel something inside you, that you haven't been made into a mere machine.

We had to get Ted over. What choice did we have? If he refused to obey the order, he'd be hauled in front of a court martial and tried as a traitor, and shot by his own people. We decided to take him with us - Owen took one arm and I took the other, and we hauled him over the top.

I'm sorry, Kit, this must be trying for you.

I can't recall everything clearly, it's as if a kind of fog descends over my memories. I'm left with bits of recollections, but the mist always seems to clear to show the bits I'd rather forget. And the noise. It's there in my ears. The roar of the guns, screams and groans, officers bellowing their orders, squeals of the shells above. But the one sound I really can't rid myself of was a horse, lying there, hit by a shell, a gash along his belly. It was such a small, gentle whinny, almost inaudible, but it stays with me, the smallest sound of all; the blood gushing out and darkening the sodden earth around it, and the warmth of it rising as steam into the air. That sound - it was the sound of the world sighing its last breath, so gentle, so final.

I remember seeing Ted's back running in front of me, his rifle stuck out in front of him. I shouted at him to wait, but he didn't, he just scrambled on. That instant there was a terrible wail as a shell exploded and splintered shards split the air, and Owen went down, hit in his side. He couldn't get up, the colour draining from his face.

Not far away, there was a crater. I dragged him into the hollow and he was groaning, his eyes searching my face. He was losing blood - there was nothing I could do, Kit. I kneeled by him, jabbering nonsense, promising him that I'd get him home, get him back to his family. It was then that Ted appeared, and the two of us crouched there in that water-logged hole, watching Owen float off. I had to do something. I had to get Owen back to the trench - he was losing too much blood, and very soon it would be too late. We had to decide: it would be hours before the stretcher bearers would venture out, and by then it would be too late. Ted took one arm, and I took the other, and we struggled up and out of the hole, and that was when the next explosion came. I remember that we were blown off our feet, and it felt as if I was moving for ages through time, and then when I crashed to earth I remember that I felt the weight of Owen's body on me. He was still and heavy. I'd made the wrong decision, Kit. Perhaps he could have been saved if I'd left him there in that hollow with Ted.

That explosion - it was so near. I recall pushing at Owen to try to release my arms. I could smell the metallic stench of blood, and damp soil, and I realised that there was a pain. I tried to reach out to feel my face, but my arms were still trapped under the weight of Owen. I tried to open my mouth, tried to shout out, to call. Then I managed to release my hand, and when I felt my face, my fingers found a void. Where my chin should have been, there was nothing there, just a flap of skin and a wetness.

From then on there was nothing but a place without light, and I remember nothing more. When I was in the train carriage on my way to hospital, I was told that it was Ted who managed to get me back to the trench, that it was Ted who made it back. One day I'd like to see him, Kit. But not now.

I don't know what became of Owen. I promised to bring him home, but I failed, and he must still be there, in the dirt in Mametz, and I've come home without him. I often think of his family, of his son - the scholar, the one who should have had the chance to get on, but now...

And here I am - sent back to you, dear Kit, a shadowy figure, hiding in the darkness. Can you take me back Kit? Can you bear to look at me and not feel pity? If it's impossible for you to think of me as your husband, I understand that. All that I want you to know is that I will always love you, my dear, and the children.

Ifor

11

I LEAVE THE letter on the bed and rush down the stairs, my legs hardly carrying me. I'm shaken, bile rising in my throat. I rush past Jim and Enid, still sitting in the doorway messing around with the coal shovel. I make it past them and into the back yard before being sick. I press my forehead on to the coolness of the stone wall, trying to steady myself.

'There.' Lora's beside me. I reach for the cup of water that she's brought: it's cold and soothing.

'I shouldn't have shown it to you, Anni. I'm sorry.'

Enid and Jim hurry after her.

'What is it, Anni? Have you been sick?' Enid stares, her eyes wide.

'It's nothing,' I gasp. 'Just a fly. I must have swallowed it!' I smile wanly. I just want to get home.

'I'm sorry, Anni.' Lora looks as if she might cry.

'I'm fine, Lora. I'll be fine.'

It feels as if I've been prying, looking at something which was not meant for my eyes – as if I had just looked in through a window at a lighted room, looked in on other people's lives. I wish I hadn't read those words, and now with my eyes shut, leaning on the wall, Ellis's face keeps returning. Not his dear face as it was this morning: his face is now the face of Owen, the soldier in Uncle Ifor's letter.

'Come on, then, Anni.' It's Enid, tugging at my arm, the other hand holding tightly on to Jim's. 'Aunty Kitty wants us to go on an errand, are you coming with us?' She looks at me, waiting.

'Where?'

'I told you, Aunty Kitty needs some yeast from Mrs Lloyd's shop. I said we could get it, come on.'

I nod and reach out for Jim's other hand. He's happy, dragging his feet, then bending his knees while Enid and I give him a swing. He squeals and laughs. I wish I could be as carefree as Jim, with no understanding of how things are in this world.

The bell attached to the shop door rings, and Jim's still laughing as we enter. The shop's dark and smells of tea and carbolic soap. Someone else is there in front of the counter, chatting with Mrs Lloyd. As my eyes adjust, I recognise the fur stole and shudder as those beady eyes clamp their stare on me. It's Gwen Jones.

She turns to take us in. Jim's still laughing as he rushes towards the counter and the colourful array of sweet jars. Gwen Jones stands to one side, as if she's afraid that Jim might knock her over in his keenness to reach the sweets.

'And how are you three little ones today?' smiles Mrs Lloyd. 'Is it one of these you're after, Jim?' She unwinds the lid off one of the jars, and hands Jim a piece of liquorice. He grabs it and puts the whole piece into his mouth, and the inky dribble froths down his chin.

'Good Lord!' Gwen Jones twists her face, and looks on in disgust. I wipe Jim's face with my hanky – after all Jim is in my charge, and I don't want to give Gwen Jones the chance to tell anyone that I didn't take my duty seriously.

'So, I hear that Ellis left this morning.' Is that a smile, or a smirk? I can't quite make it out. But I know the eyes of the fox are scowling at me.

'Ellis?' Mrs Lloyd comes round to this side, her hands plucking at her apron, 'Dear Lord, has Ellis gone? Not Ellis, surely? Do they need Ellis too?' Mrs Lloyd clearly hadn't heard.

'What will become of us without Ellis? Who'll be leading the concert next week, then?'

I don't really care who'll be conducting the concert, but I know what she means, and I want to thank her for it. Gwen Jones sniffs, but Mrs Lloyd goes on, 'And what about his poems, and his work, and your poor father, Anni? How will he get along without Ellis there to help?' She returns the lid to the jar and puts it back on the shelf, tut-tutting to herself. 'This horrible war,' she mutters. 'It just keeps on stealing our boys, and now it's taking Ellis away...'

'Huh! Ellis will just have to do what all the other lads have already done, Mrs Lloyd. There are far more important duties when Lloyd George calls on you to defend king and country. I don't think writing rhymes will help the war effort, somehow.'

Gwen Jones and the fox fur turn on their heel, and the bell jingles as the door bangs shut behind them.

Mrs Lloyd smiles apologetically and squeezes herself back behind the counter.

'What can I get you, my dears?'

'An ounce of yeast for Aunty Kitty, please,' Enid says, and Mrs Lloyd disappears between the thick curtains at the back. I look around at the cluster of jars, their glittering contents illuminating the darkness, and I remember about the promise I made to get Enid a special present. It's just then that I notice a small velvet purse on the edge of the counter. Jim and Enid are still mesmerised by the sweet jars. Suddenly I've got hold of the purse and I've put it in my apron pocket, just as Mrs Lloyd comes back through the curtain into the shop. I tug at my coat to cover my apron, but in an instant I feel my cheeks burning and I want to put the purse back on the counter – but I know it's too late. Mrs Lloyd hands Enid the small packet of yeast and puts a note in her account book, and Enid gives her the money.

'Well, tell Aunty Kitty that I'm asking after her, and give my regards to your mother, girls. Tell her that I shall come up to

Yr Ysgwrn one of these days.' She bids us goodbye, and the bell screeches its accusation as the door shuts behind us.

The purse is in my pocket, burning at the material just like a hot ember. I can feel it scorching my skin.

I can see Lora at the top of the street. I suppose she's on her way to meet us, but then she stops and looks towards the side street. She's waiting for someone. Someone approaches her, with his back towards us. It's Huw. I watch the two, and a pang of something hits my stomach. From here I can't hear the conversation, but they're both in good spirits, laughing and bantering.

Jim's poking about in the hedge – there's a robin in there, scratching. When I look again, Huw's handing something to Lora, and I notice the way she has her head to one side, that little gesture that I know means she's a little smug. Whatever it is, she's pleased, and she puts it in her pocket.

It's then that she notices us approaching. They exchange glances – I can't make out what passes between them, but Huw leaves, hurrying back along the side street and out of my view. Laura reaches us. I can tell she's pleased and she has that air about her.

'Was that Huw?' I ask, although I know.

She smiles, a shy smile, almost apologising.

'Yes.' She puts her hand in her pocket as if to check on whatever's in there. And then I think of the contents of my pocket – my heart dips, and I feel sick again. Just then Wil comes along.

'Heard Ellis went this morning. On the first train, was it?' He clears his throat: he has more to say. 'He'll be off to France, you see – straight out there. Our boys are winning, and they just need more soldiers to get it done right and proper – finish the job. So he'll be on the next ship over to France, you see, Anni.'

How does Wil Ferret know all these things? I don't stop to

think, I just give him a shove, and somehow he loses his footing and falls backwards into the ditch. The ditch where Mr Lloyd's just emptied the slurry from clearing out the horses. Wil just sits there in the muck, a stunned look on his face.

Lora grabs hold of Jim's hand, and I clutch at Enid's arm, and we run for our lives.

12

I TAKE THE velvet purse out from under the mattress. It sits there on the bedclothes as if it's alive. The small neat stitches are perfect, forming curving patterns along the edges. I despise that purse.

When Enid's birthday came, I gave her a lace flower – Maggie helped make it – and she also got a poem from Ellis, who hadn't forgotten, and Mam made a towering pile of pancakes for tea, although I only managed to eat one. That's weeks back by now, but knowing the purse is there under the mattress makes me want to crawl somewhere dark and hide.

All's well with Ellis: Wil apparently knows nothing of the war effort, because Ellis is still in Litherland, and sends letters often, telling us about the soldiers he's met. So many of them have connections we know. But I'm miserable. Things are not as they should be between Lora and me.

I don't know what it is. She doesn't tell me things like she used to. I know she's busy, helping her mother, and she's stopped attending school since her father came back home. It's strange at school without her. Wil Ferret's the only one the same age as me – all the other pupils are younger. The older ones have left: they need to work and help their families. I want to leave school, but Mam insists I stay, saying I'm too young to go out to work as I'm not quite 14 yet.

I called by Lora's house yesterday, thinking perhaps we could go for a walk, or perhaps sneak upstairs and have a chat. Lora said she couldn't because she was too busy helping, so I started heading home, but just then I looked back and saw her leaving the house. I thought she'd changed her mind and was going to hurry after me, but instead she turned the other way, and I saw Huw coming to meet her.

I feel a churning inside me when I think of it – it's like a betrayal. It was me who spoke to Huw first when we went to the Band o'Hope, not Lora. Perhaps it was just that he happened to be on the street yesterday, I try to convince myself, and they just chanced to see each other. But then a scathing voice inside my head says I'm a fool: of course it wasn't just lady luck.

I take another glance at the velvet purse. Then something comes to me – a notion, a thought. Of course: that's it. It's the purse. The first time I saw Huw and Lora together was the day I stole the purse. Those stitches are just like eyes, evil eyes watching me, leering at me. Could it be that the purse is a bad omen? A force that brings bad luck? No, it's more than bad luck – it causes everything to go topsy-turvy, somehow. Nothing's like it should be. I'm being punished for my sin. It's like when I have to pick up those quartz stones, because leaving them on the ground will risk causing something bad to happen. Now, because I have this cursed purse in my possession, I've somehow brought all this down upon me.

My mind's racing. What other awful events can happen now that this purse is sitting there cursing me? Maggie's on her way back from a neighbour's – surely nothing bad can happen to her? Then Ifan and Bob are out collecting wood with the horse and cart: what if the horses bolt and drag the boys with them? The horses are old and quiet, and Bob and Ifan can handle them, so I think it's unlikely. Ellis! It's Ellis – he's in the camp, where guns and ammunition can go off at any minute. Anything could happen to him. I think my blood's turned to ice – I can hardly breathe. I grab the purse, and wrap it in a piece of paper. I have to give it back. I have to be rid of it.

I run most of the way. Gasping for breath, I reach the shop. My hair's escaped from underneath my cap and the wind's whipped it, so it's tangled and unruly. I look about me, hoping and praying that no one's about. Dusk's reaching into the corners. I have to hurry, but I need to check that no one's in the shop, so I peer in through the window. The coast is clear. Luckily the door's ajar, so the bell doesn't ring as I push it open gently. I take the paper parcel out of my pocket. I'll be able to leave it there at the edge of the counter, and no one need know. I hurry to unwrap the purse, trying to breathe calmly, my heartbeat booming in my ears. It's just as I'm about to push the purse on to the wooden counter that the bell jangles, and I jump. Someone's entered – it's Gwen Jones. I can hear Mrs Lloyd approaching from behind the thick curtain, and I know that the net has fallen and I'm caught, red handed.

'What have you there?' Gwen Jones asks, slithering towards me, her eyes darting.

'That's a neat hand of embroidery.' She peers at the purse. 'You didn't make it, did you? Is it your purse, Anni?'

She knows it isn't mine. This is a small treasure, a dainty, crimson velvet purse, delicate stitches embroidered along its edges. Where would I get hold of a purse like this?

Mrs Lloyd comes to the edge of the counter. She takes a look at Gwen Jones, and then her eyes rest on me – she has a curious look on her face. I'm lost. I want to cry – I can feel the panic rising inside me, like bile. My throat is scorched, the words disappearing as soon as they reach the tip of my tongue. All I can think of is the word *thief*. I'm a *thief*. Another wave of panic chokes me. Everyone will find out: Mam and Tada, sitting there by the hearth, looking at me with disappointed, disbelieving eyes. Ellis – his smile vanishing – and Enid, Maggie, Bob and Ifan – how will they bear to have me at home?

Mrs Lloyd reaches out for the purse and turns it over and over in her hands.

'Well? Is it your purse, Anni Evans?' Gwen Jones is right beside me, accusing. 'Where did *you* get hold of something as pretty as this, I wonder? It cost a penny or two, I'd say. Or did you just take it, Anni? Did you just try and hide it behind your back when I came in just now?'

I feel the floor rushing up at me. Will I go to prison? Is there a prison for girls my age, or –

'Thank you, Anni – will you tell Maggie that I'm pleased with it? It's beautiful, don't you think, Mrs Jones?' Mrs Lloyd looks at me, and smiles.

'Yes,' I stammer; my face crimson, matching the wretched purse.

I understand. Relief floods over me, and I steady myself. Mrs Lloyd – dear Mrs Lloyd! – has come to my defence.

'Go on through, Anni,' she continues, pulling the curtain to one side, bidding me to take the route to safety. Then she turns to Gwen Jones. 'It was Maggie - she got it in Liverpool for me when she was last over there, you see... now then, what can I get you, Mrs Jones?'

I'm still shaking when Mrs Lloyd comes through. The shop bell rings and I sigh, knowing that Gwen Jones has left at last.

She points to the chair, and I sit.

'Are you feeling better, Anni?' she asks. 'The colour's coming back to your face now.'

'I'm so sorry, Mrs Lloyd...' I try, but the tears choke me – I'm so ashamed. Mrs Lloyd waits patiently for my tears to subside, and for me to blow my nose. I start to explain, and somehow I'm telling her about all my woes. I tell her of my promise to Enid. I tell her about Lora, who's always been my best friend, but has now become a stranger. I tell her about my habit of collecting quartz stones to protect me from all calamities, and I tell her of the curse of the crimson purse, and the hold its evil eye has over me.

I blurt everything out without stopping.

'...and now both Mam and Tada will be so disappointed.'

Mrs Lloyd remains seated across from me until my blabbering has finished. She passes me a hanky and looks straight at me, her eyes quite serious.

'Anni, you know that you've done wrong, but I think that you've been shaken enough by your silly mistake, so we need not talk of it again.'

'I'm sorry.'

'But you must understand that what becomes of us is not always ruled by us. Sometimes fate plays its part – what will be, will be: whether we're to live or die, whether we're to be rich or poor, happy or unhappy. It has nothing to do with picking quartz stones out of the mud or leaving them where they are. It has nothing to do with bad omens or luck – no object brings bad luck, you see. You're a clever girl, Anni. Don't let stupidity rule you. There'll be times when things happen – they may be happy, they may be sad – but those happenings very often can't be ruled by our doings. They call that fate, I suppose, and we must sometimes accept that.'

She cocks her head to one side and smiles wanly, before going on: 'But there are choices we can make too, you see. You can choose to be fair or unfair, kind or unkind, honest or dishonest. These are choices that we are able to make. You made the wrong choice when you took that purse, Anni, but you chose to take it just the same. We aren't cursed by objects like that purse, Anni – that would be superstition. It just felt that way, because your conscience started to trouble you.'

Then she stopped again and her face was solemn. 'But you made another decision – you decided to return the purse. You made a choice: you brought it back. I don't know why you decided to do that – only you know that – but you returned what was not rightly yours.'

She gets out of her chair and pats me on the shoulder.

'Do you understand?' she asks. I nod, and she goes on. 'Some things we can't rule – we can do nothing to make them happen or prevent them from happening. But sometimes we do have the opportunity to make decisions, to choose the path. That's when we must use our judgement, and be wise. Promise me, Anni, that you'll always try to choose wisely.'

I get up and smile and nod energetically, relief making me light-headed.

'I don't expect you'll make many unwise choices, Anni.'

'Do you think so?' I'm not as confident as Mrs Lloyd is of my judgement.

'Of course I am. Now dry those tears.' I follow her into the shop, and she reaches out for the liquorice jar, and hands me a piece. 'Now then, can you do something for me?' she asks.

I dry my eyes and thank her for the liquorice, as she hands me a package.

'It will save my legs a bit – can you take it up to Aunty Kitty for me?'

'Of course I can, Mrs Lloyd, and thank you,' I gush. I would have gone on an errand all the way to Blaenau Ffestiniog – anywhere.

'Thank you, Anni.' She turns back and disappears behind the thick curtain. I run out into the street, the bell singing behind me. There's a damp drizzle outside, the kind of drizzle that gets into your eyes and between the layers of your clothes, but I don't care. It's lovely! I run up the street towards Lora's house, and the weight off my shoulders makes me feel as if I'm flying.

13

LORA OPENS THE door, and stands to one side. I go past her into the warm kitchen, where Aunty Kitty stands by the table cutting the loaf into paper-thin slices. The door to the back bedroom's open, I notice, but Jim keeps as far as possible from the darkened room. He scampers to greet me, grabbing hold of my coat and yanking me towards the table.

'No,' I try. 'I'm not staying.'

'Anni, how are you all? Where have you been hiding?' Aunty Kitty gives a little chuckle, and moves so that I can come to the table.

'We're all fine, thanks, Aunty Kitty, but please don't let me trouble you. I'm really not staying, thank you – I must be off home, but Mrs Lloyd gave me this to bring you.'

I give her the little package.

'From Mrs Lloyd? Thanks, Anni.' She takes the package.

I smile shyly at Lora, and she returns my smile.

'Have something to eat.' Aunty Kitty puts the bread on a plate, and pushes it towards me. 'There's some syrup there, look.'

Then she takes a plate through to the back bedroom, and I hear my name mentioned in a hushed voice. She returns.

'Ifor's asking after Ellis – how are things at the camp? Will he have to leave soon? Will he be home to help with the ploughing, Anni? Farm lads are sometimes given leave to help, aren't they?'

'I don't know, Aunty Kitty. I haven't heard anything.'

'Well, they need all hands on deck for ploughing, you know, what with the war effort and everything.' Aunty Kitty obviously knows about these things. The fire seems to be casting a much rosier tint on to my world just now. I hope Aunty Kitty's right – having Ellis home would make everything glow.

'Anyway, Ellis is fine, thanks. He just complains about the dampness of the camp, and the cold. We can't keep up with his constant demand for socks and scarves,' I laugh. 'Mam thinks he probably shares them out with all the other lads, or else he keeps on leaving them somewhere.'

'I hear that Litherland is cold – it's the River Mersey, bringing sea mist in with it,' says Aunty Kitty, and returns her attention to the loaf.

'How's school?' Lora asks. She looks at me awkwardly, and smiles – we're strangers. How can this be? When did it happen?

Then she gives me a sly poke, and points to the front door. I understand, and get to my feet.

'Well, I must be going, Aunty Kitty,' I say, knowing that my manners are shoddy. I haven't even quite managed to swallow what's left of my bread and syrup.

'Yes, Anni – you take care on your way. Give your mother my regards, and if you hear anything from Ellis, come over. Ifor would like to know what he's up to.'

I ruffle Jim's hair, and wait as Lora pulls on her coat.

'Where are you off to, Lora?' Aunty Kitty looks at Lora, and hesitates: she has more to say.

'I'll just see Anni off, Mam. I'll just go as far as the bridge.' Aunty Kitty nods, but she's not pleased. I can't make it out. Why wouldn't she be? Lora always comes with me for part of my way home.

'Come straight back, then, Lora,' she says, and her voice is sharp.

Outside, the rain's stopped but the fog envelopes us, muffling our voices, stifling the sound of our steps.

'Is everything well...?' I venture, '...at home? Do you miss school, Lora?'

'Yes, I mean... Everything's fine at home, but sometimes I miss the banter, you know, at school... when we... Well, I miss the conversations we had on our way home and... you know, Anni.'

Her voice was duller somehow, it didn't have that lightness to it. She didn't sound like Lora Margaret.

'Is it your Tada? But he's getting better isn't he? How's Jim with him now?' I didn't know how to ask, how to get her to talk, and I didn't want to pry. I didn't usually have to ask her anything, because I knew all her answers. I knew her inside out. That's how it used to be. I should let her talk.

'No, it's not Tada. He *is* getting better, I suppose, or I'm getting used to things as they are. Jim isn't though – he won't go near Tada, and hides if Tada comes out to sit with us... It's difficult. It makes us all sad to see the way he reacts, and Mam – well, she got cross with him yesterday. She raised her voice and he was sent to bed.'

'Aunty Kitty did that?' I couldn't imagine her being angry with Jim – she has the patience of a saint.

'Yes, well... Then she couldn't bear it, thinking of Jim up in bed all alone, his breath coming in jerks through his tears. In the end she went to fetch Jim down again, and it was Tada who had to retreat – he went back into the back bedroom, out of sight.'

Laura looks at me sadly, and I rush to grab her arm. I think she might cry. Then she stops suddenly, and I almost trip. She swings round to face me, and her eyes are wide.

'I've got something to tell you, Anni, but you have to promise to keep it a secret.'

Her face looks so strained, it must be something terrible. Is she ill? My heart lurches, and I can hardly breathe.

'Promise?' she whispers.

'Of course I promise,' I nod. 'Aren't I your best friend?'

'Yes, you are, Anni.'

'Well?'

Lora pauses, and a wide smile erupts and her face is almost illuminated.

'I'm going to be married, Anni! Huw and me – we're getting married!'

'What?!'

What does she mean? She can't get married! She can't get married – after all, she's only a year older than me. Almost 15 – that's far too young to be married, and she's only just met Huw. It's ridiculous!

'You can't!' I blurt out. 'You can't get married, surely?'

'Why?' Lora's smiling at me.

'Because, because... well, what about your Mam? Doesn't she need your help?'

The smile disappears. Lora's face hardens.

'Mam!' Lora snorts, 'I don't want to think about Mam!'

I stare at her. She doesn't sound like Lora Margaret.

'Why can't Huw and me get married? Not just yet, I know that, but when I'm older – 16, perhaps. He'll have been working for a quite few months as a farm hand by then. I've got £5, you know Anni – Taid Minffordd left me the money, and I've got it saved: a whole £5 note. Anyway, I've heard that they need housemaids in Rhiwgoch, so I'm going there to ask about a place soon – will you come with me, Anni?'

She clutches at my hands, and pulls me towards her, her eyes wide and excited.

'Mam doesn't know, Anni – you won't tell, will you?' she pleads with me. 'Because I can't tell her, not with Tada the way he is now.'

'Of course I won't tell, Lora, but...' I can't be cross with her, but it doesn't make sense. 'What about Huw's family though? I thought he had to work to help his mother and young brother... Does she know about your plan?'

'No, not yet. Huw hasn't been home since before Christmas.

He doesn't want to go home because it's such a sad place, I suppose. His mother still believes that his father's alive, because they didn't find a body. She still expects him to come in through the door... She's convinced he's out there in France or somewhere with his mind gone, not knowing who he is or where he comes from... Do you think it's possible, Anni?'

'I don't know,' I reply.

Suddenly dark shapes come up the street towards us, their heads down, deep in conversation. They loom up through the mist, almost knocking into us before they realise we're here.

'Promise me you won't tell?" Lora hisses, just as my brother Ifan and Huw reach us.

'Anni!' Ifan's laughing and grabbing at my arm. I try to shake him off – he doesn't usually want anything to do with me; ignoring me, as brothers do.

'Anni, come on – Ellis has come home!'

'What?'

'Come on! He came home on the six o'clock train, hurry!'

'But –'

'He's on leave.'

I start to run – or perhaps I'm flying after Ifan down through the silent streets, I'm so elated. Then I remember Lora's words. I stop and turn: I can just make out Lora and Huw, standing there where we left them. I shout into the mist:

'Lora, I promise...'

14

A UNTY KITTY WAS right. Ellis is allowed home for the ploughing, as are many of other farm lads here in Trawsfynydd. All of a sudden there's a lightness to our days, relief making us all laugh louder, our step almost weightless – a burden lifted from us. Ellis is at home at last. We're almost giddy with the happiness of it. Everything's changed, somehow – Tada's arthritis is better, and Mam's face has soothed, the frown almost gone. Enid and me aren't sent to school, as there's so much to get done on the farm. I seem to be fetching water all day, or there's baking to be done or milk to be churned. Even the weather's settled, and every night I stand in the yard looking at the clouds turning pink and crimson over the mountains, and I know that the sea beyond them must be alight with the sun dipping into it. The other night I was allowed to go with Ellis part of the way down to the mill, which is where he meets his friends, and where they catch up and put the world to rights – what there is left of the old crowd. Most of them are away fighting, of course. I stopped nearby for a while and listened to the far-off sound of their banter and laughter, feeling warm and content. Everything's so much better when Ellis is at home.

Jini Owen comes over to Yr Ysgwrn often these days. Mam must like her very much, because when Jini's planning a visit then Mam takes so much trouble baking and cooking. It's as if one of the gentry's visiting, and we tease Mam about it, and we're not told off. Of course we're all pleased to welcome Jini – she's kind and pretty, and I think Ellis is in love, truly in love. Last week when she came, he left his writing, and walked with Jini up to the top fields, and Enid saw him give her a posy of primroses. Then he walked her all the way home to Blaenau Festiniog, and we were all in bed before he got back.

Today when I got up, he was at the table working on his *awdl*, but he had to clear everything as we crowded into the kitchen.

I find a copy of one of his poems – it had slipped on to the floor flags, probably as Maggie and Ellis rushed to clear most of the papers away so that Mam could set the table for breakfast. I sit on the bench, reading the scrawled writing. It's a poem entitled 'Gwenfron and I', and it's a story in the form of a poem. It's a simple poem, and I understand it – it tells of two sweethearts who are able to enjoy the path of life together, and it ends with both of them in old age, their backs bowed but still in love. I think it's beautiful.

Gwenfron and I

Gwenfron and I strolled together one day,
As, high in the branches, a breeze laughed away;
A moon shone above, a moon shone in the lake,
A nightingale sang in the valley brake,
Such a night as when love is most awake;
And there, as the breeze and the stream murmured by,
We made a firm covenant, Gwenfron and I.

Many years later, when the bare trees below
In the valley were stilled under whitest snow,
The hours of youth had fled evermore,
And everywhere filled with cares by the score,
And the hurricane raged from the woods with a roar,
Be the winter so bitter, let the floods thunder by;
That covenant holds between Gwenfron and I.

Gwenfron and I are aged by now,
and hoary of head like the whitest snow.
Our eyes are grown dim as the evening light,
Our muscles have wasted, our strength become slight:
But see how our love still increases in might.
To the lands beyond aging we go, by and by,
And quietly cross the stream, Gwenfron and I.

I read and reread it. And it comes to me that this is what Ellis has been dreaming of: meeting someone special. Will it be Jini? Will he find love, share his life with her – the happy times and sad, raise a family perhaps, and grow old together? Is this what we all want? Is it possible, or is it too much to ask for? That's all Ellis is seeking, a life just like Tada and Mam have, and I can only thank the Lord that Uncle Ifor's come home so he and Aunty Kitty can grow old together, too. And that's when I realise that all those lads, many of them Ellis's friends, won't have the opportunity to do just that. They won't come home – they're lost and sunk in a dark earth in places with names that we've never heard of. They won't come home to their sweethearts, wives, mothers or sisters, and those of us at home will age, and our memory of them will be forever young – but in a cruel way. They've lost the chance of a life of normality, the chance to do all those small deeds that we do in our lives. It's not much – but it's life.

I want to show Lora the poem because it's about what she's longing for too, and sitting here on the bench with the poem in my hand, I realise I'm not cross with her for wanting to marry Huw. I suppose that's how things are when you fall in love.

Of course Ellis was allowed home on leave to help with the ploughing. The country needs to produce more potatoes, oats – all kinds of crops for the war effort. It's a busy time, and everyone's out there in the fields helping prepare them for planting – everyone except Ellis. He's stuck inside, his head bowed, fountain pen poised. He has to finish the *awdl* before his leave's over, because he needs to send it to the competition soon. It's Tada who's keenest, and Jini too, saying that this is his chance to win the top prize at the Eisteddfod – the Chair. I think writing a long ode like the *awdl* must be harder than ploughing, seeing the furrows on Ellis's face, and sometimes he looks up and shakes his head, gesturing that he's going to to give up on it. Then Tada reminds him that he was second for the Chair prize last year, when the Eisteddfod was at Aberystwyth, and that we're really in need of a new chair as the one he sits in is riddled with woodworm. But he's only joking – you can't really sit in an Eisteddfod Chair, they're huge clumsy things, all carved with decorated patterns, and it would be hard to squeeze one into our small kitchen. So Ellis sits, thinking of his *awdl*, but Jini's on her way here today, and they'll go out for a while.

It's a beautiful spring day at Yr Ysgwrn, and this is the only place on earth I want to be. The cuckoo has arrived, and is up there in the copse in the back field, proclaiming its return, and in the cowshed the house martins dart in and out, swooping by and just missing our heads. Clumps of primroses appear along the base of the rough stone walls, as if strewn there by a careless old wizard. The lambs, strengthened now by the increasing warmth of a new sun, have been herded with their mothers up on to the mountain pasture. They scamper and race along the edge of the slope, silhouetted against the pale blue sky.

When Jini comes, Ellis puts his papers to one side. Mam comes through from the back kitchen with a basket of food, which she passes to Ellis.

'Where will you go?' Mam asks.

They don't know where they're off to – those kind of details aren't important – but Jini has a rosy glow on her face, and I see why Ellis is just a little besotted. Jini's beautiful in a shy, modest way, not at all bold or forward. Her dark eyes have a spark in them, and her lips seem to hold a ready smile that will light up her face at any minute, and make everyone around her want to smile too. That's how she is – that's Jini Owen, who will one day be welcomed into our family as our sister, I hope.

'Where shall we head?' Ellis asks, grabbing his jacket from the back of the chair.

'We'll just follow our noses,' Jini laughs, and reaches out for the basket from Ellis. She thanks Mam.

I so want to join them: they're young, full of life and laughter, and the world's smiling at them. When Jini's around, Ellis seems to forget about his poetry, and the war, for a while at least.

'Ellis, can I –' but I can see the warning in my mother's eyes, and I falter.

Ellis turns and smiles at me.

'Not today, Anni. But I promise, when I come home for good – you know, when the war's over – then I'll take you to Barmouth: Enid, Maggie, Mam and you.' He turns to Jini. 'Will you join us, Jini? We'll take a towel, and we can dip our feet in the sea.' He smiles, and they're off. I run out to the yard and watch them as they go. Ellis comments on something that makes Jini giggle. They pause – they're both laughing, their faces bright, reflecting the light. Two lovers out walking, and the sun shining.

These are contented days, and Yr Ysgwrn is where all of us want to be.

15

'I JUST DON'T understand. Mam won't give me a reason – she just refuses to discuss it.' Lora's eyes fill up again, and she insists on dabbing fiercely at her nose with her hanky, so it's as red as her eyes. I want to remind her that a red, sniffing nose is an unbecoming look for any young girl, and if she insists on rubbing it like that, she does risk it staying crimson forever and ever, amen. But thankfully something about her wailing warns me that it would be unwise to remind her of that. I don't think she wants to hear my views on crimson noses today, as it seems she may have to rethink this marriage thing with Huw, and might well have to look elsewhere for a husband.

All this crying is because Aunty Kitty doesn't approve of Huw. But it doesn't make sense, because Aunty Kitty will never say anything bad about anyone. Well, almost anyone. I can't imagine Huw doing or saying anything that might make her dislike him – not like Gwen Jones, who Aunty Kitty once called a slithering snake.

'What did she say, Lora?' I try to get her to calm down, because she's making no sense, and the hiccuping's making her words come out all muddled.

'She said I mustn't see him again, and she said... H-Huw...' – but the tears start again, and the nose rubbing – '...and she said I shouldn't even ment-mention his name, because it upsets Tada... and when he hears H-Huw's name he gets so upset he goes back into that dark place he was at... you know, in his mind.'

'But why?' I can't understand it either. It's so out of character for Aunty Kitty.

'I don't know, Anni. Huw hasn't done anything... I haven't

done anything... and I don't understand why Huw's name should upset Tada so much.'

'Does Uncle Ifor know about Huw's father, and all that worry?' I try to untie the thoughts that form knots in my mind. There must be a reason why Huw's name upsets Uncle Ifor like that. There has to be an explanation, but what is it?

'Yes, he knows Huw's father's missing. I thought that would be a reason for Mam and Tada to welcome him in with open arms, but it isn't like that, and I can't understand it. He's forbidden to call on me...' – the hanky starts rubbing again – ' and now I'm not allowed to go out to meet him, or even to mention his name.'

I try to soothe her, hugging and rocking her as we did when we were small and one of us had bashed a knee on a wall or something. Eventually the tears dry. Lora sniffs one last sniff, and straightens, her chin high.

'Do I have a red nose, Anni?' she asks, smoothing her hair. She has an almost wild look about her.

'No, of course not,' I lie.

'Well, I'm not going to listen or take heed this time, Anni, because this time Mam's wrong.' She looks as if she could take on the whole of the German Army just now. I feel uneasiness gnawing at me: I know Lora, and if she decides on one path, then steering her on to another is not an easy task.

'I won't be listening to Mam. Poor Huw, he's already lost his father. I'm not turning my back on him now, Anni.'

'No...' I reply, but wasn't sure if I'd just nodded in agreement, or if I'd just questioned her with a 'No?'

My answer doesn't seem to worry Lora either way. I don't think she hears or interprets the 'no'.

'Will you help me, Anni?' She has a plan – I can tell. Suddenly she's taking something out of her coat pocket: it's an envelope. She kisses it, and holds it out to me.

'Will you take this to Huw, please?' She's smiling sadly at me now. 'Please?'

I don't know what to say. What should I do? I stand staring at the letter in her outstretched hand. I have to choose. I remember Mrs Lloyd's words about stealing the purse.

'Promise me, Anni, that you'll always try to choose wisely.'

But what should I do now? Aunty Kitty and Uncle Ifor are wise and kind. Aunty Kitty's always been someone I can turn to for help or support, and now I'm supposed to go behind her back. It feels like a terrible betrayal of her kindness. But Lora's my best friend, and I know that Huw isn't a bad influence on her – he's polite and well mannered, and they just want to be happy together. I stand, and wonder if I'm visibly shifting from one foot to the other, or whether it's just in my mind.

I'm not sure Lora's thought this out properly. From what I can gather, she has this great notion in her head of what life will be like when she and Huw are married. But after all, Huw's only a farm hand – it's not as if she's managed to land Lloyd George's son, as we'd dreamed. All of a sudden, I wish we'd never met Huw on that fateful night – never set eyes on him. Things will never be the same between me and Lora Margaret, and it's Huw's fault, I suppose. And then an idea sprouts in my mind: is this the chance I need to get Lora back as my true best friend, without Huw edging in between us? Huw would get over Lora, wouldn't he? After all, he'd be busy with his work at Frongoch, so he probably wouldn't have much time to mull over the disappearance of Lora Margaret from his life. He might just stay over there, and be out of our lives altogether.

I take the letter from her and put it in my coat pocket.

'You will take the letter, won't you, Anni?' Had she seen that little seed growing, taking root in my head?

'You will take it?' she asks again. 'Please don't forget. I want him to know I haven't turned my back on him, that it isn't anything he's done.'

'No, Lora,' I whisper. 'I won't forget.'

Lora gives my hand a little squeeze. 'Thanks, Anni.' And she's gone, clambering over the wall. I struggle up on to the stile, my coat tripping me, and watch her go. She doesn't run like she usually does, she dawdles, her shoulders slumped, her eyes searching the floor as she goes. I know – she doesn't want to go home.

I jump down from the stile. I have a gnawing inside me. I feel for the letter in my pocket, take it out and study it. The paper of the envelope's thin and I try to make out some of the words through it, but I can't. I've reached the bridge, and I look over its parapet and watch the dark pool below. A small, flimsy leaf is taken by the water: it gets swirled around by an eddy, before getting stuck on the rocks. I watch, willing it to be dislodged, and it is – another rush of water takes it away. It'll be far, far away, perhaps out to the sea, by sunset.

I hold the letter above the water, over the parapet. If I drop it now, then no one will know – it'll simply be taken, swirled and tossed by the rush of water, and Lora's words will fade away.

'You have a choice, Anni.' It's Mrs Lloyd's voice; it's my voice, whispering through my thoughts.

Lora's my best friend, and Huw doesn't deserve to lose her – he's suffered enough losses.

I push the letter back into my pocket, and run. I run until I reach the house, and then I bang on the door. Huw's there.

'Here it is,' I blurt. 'It's your letter.'

Then I'm gone.

16

ALL OF US knew those hazy, heady days would come to an end. Ellis went back after his ploughing leave, and the camp at Litherland did its work. The training's done now and the latest batch of boys is transformed, it seems, into soldiers. Ellis too is a soldier, and he's joined the Royal Welsh Fusiliers with the other lads at the camp, swapping his rake for a rifle. He managed to snatch another few days at home, just one final short leave before... well, I don't want to think about that. But sadly these last few long, warm evenings of early summer when we've watched the moon's reflection in the pool at the end of the pasture, when Ellis is still a poet and words his only weapon, have disappeared all too quickly. We all knew we couldn't keep him here with us. It was only leave, after all.

It's the evening before he leaves for Litherland again, and Jini's come. It's a beautiful evening – one of those evenings when I'm afraid to breathe in case I somehow cause the magic to dissolve in front of my eyes. The sky's a brilliant cobalt, and all around me the mountains and pastures seem to shimmer purple, green and gold. There's no breeze, and the leaves in the orchard are motionless. My world is still, and waiting.

I'm making Maggie's bed by the open window when Ellis and Jini come out into the front yard, just below me.

'I'll walk with you part of the way.' Ellis waits for her by the gate.

'No, stay,' she says, and turns to face him. 'You have enough to keep you busy. I can easily cross the river by the stepping stones, then I'll be on time to get the last train.'

Ellis mumbles, and I have to move closer to the window so that I can hear his words. He stands with his back to me, and his head's bowed. I can see that Jini's struggling, but she's trying to be brave.

'You will write, when you get to Litherland?' she ventures. 'Perhaps... well, perhaps – you know, they won't send you straight out there. You might be allowed to stay at the camp for a while.'

'No.' Ellis's voice is low, and hesitant, as if he doesn't want to crush her hopes. 'No, it's time for our lot to join the battalion now, Jini. I have to face it at last – I expect to be in France by next week.'

I have to turn my face away – looking at Jini's too hard. She's just like all the rest of us, clutching at any hope, just trying to think of a lifeline – but we know there isn't one.

'I'll write and let you know.' He reaches for both her hands, and pulls her to him. They stand there in the yard, holding each other.

'But when I come back...' He looks into her face, but she has her eyes downcast. 'When I come back, you will be here, Jini Owen, won't you? You will wait for me?' He's teasing, trying to lighten things, but his voice is strained. 'And when September comes, will you come with me to Birkenhead, to fetch my Eisteddfod prize? We'll have to put the chair on the train to bring it back here to Yr Ysgwrn.'

'Yes, I'll come with you,' she smiles wanly. 'But you must promise to finish it properly, and send it in on time. I know you, Ellis! You're so absent minded – don't leave it all scrunched up in your kit bag!'

They stand there, holding on to each other: just lovers, not wanting to part. But they don't hold their destiny. Like Mrs Lloyd said, sometimes we can choose for ourselves, but at other times the choice is made by others and we have no say in it. They have no say in it, no say at all. They stand there for a long time, and then Jini raises her hands to Ellis's face and kisses him.

'I'll pray for you, pray that you come back safely. And I'll be just here, Ellis,' she says, scuffing a mark in the dust with her foot. 'Just here, waiting for you.'

I have to turn away then. How much more parting must I witness? I climb into Maggie's bed and hide under the bedcover, but I know I can't hide here forever.

17

'ANNI!' THE VOICE comes from the direction of the river. 'Anni, wait for me!' It's Wil Ferret, rushing to meet me. I'm on my way to the shop – I have to fetch some soap for Mam. I stare at the ground and plough onwards, pretending not to hear.

'Wait, Anni!' He shouts so loudly I have to stop, because others have started to stare in our direction, and I don't want Wil to make more of a spectacle. He careers across the road, over the stile, and is at my side.

'Are you on your way to the village?' he asks, awkwardly.

'Of course I am. Where else would I be going this way?' Immediately I wish I hadn't sounded so cross. I'm hurrying on, and Wil's struggling to keep up with me.

'I'm going that way too.' He's lying – he was heading the other way – but I don't question him.

'Have you heard from Ellis?' he asks.

'Yes.'

'Oh?'

I don't want to tell him more.

'Is he... is he all right, Anni?'

I stop – there's a change in Wil's questioning. He doesn't seem quite himself. I look closely at him, and he looks seriously at me – is that concern? I can't quite make it out.

'Where's Ellis now, Anni? Is he still at the camp in Liverpool?' He has his head cocked to one side.

'No.'

'Oh.'

I walk on, poised, expecting the next flurry of questions. Wil walks beside me, but no more questions come. Something strange has happened to Wil since I last saw him. Just then he pauses, and turns to watch the men over in the field cutting the hay, their scythes swishing in a steady rhythm. The settled weather seems as if it's here to stay, so all the farmers are keen to finish the haymaking. I wait with Wil, watching. If he has any gossip or a story about one of the workers over in the field, he chooses not to share it. Then he starts off again, and I realise the silence is even more unnerving than Wil's usual questions. We walk on, to just the sound of our feet on the dusty road.

'Ellis is in France now,' I crack. 'He's somewhere near a place called Ro-something – Rouen, I think.'

'Oh, yes, that's a long way from any fighting, Anni – well, I think it is, anyway.' But he doesn't stop. 'He'll be fine, Anni. He probably won't have to go to the front, even.'

He smiles at me, and I nod. I think he just wants to be nice, trying to reassure me like that, because of course he doesn't know where Rouen is. And he knows that I know he doesn't know.

'Perhaps you're right, Wil,' is all I can say.

Letters come regularly from Ellis. His battalion sailed from Southampton and reached a place called Le Havre, in France, and then they went on to that place called Rouen. Ellis doesn't tell us much about the camp, but he's very good at describing the countryside. He says we would like France; that it's very pretty, with tall, slim trees and the delicate leaves rustling in the breeze. Tada thinks the trees may be poplars, but we don't have them in Trawsfynydd. Although Ellis mainly writes about the beauty of the countryside, he did mention being woken one night by the sound of the guns from far off, thudding and groaning. I don't think I ever want to go there.

I turn to Wil. 'It's sweltering there, you know, in France.'

'Does Ellis like the hot weather?' he asks.

'I suppose so. He doesn't complain, anyway.' I laugh, 'He doesn't want any more scarves!'

Ellis did a little sketch in his last letter: a small matchstick soldier, wearing thick gloves and a huge scarf around its neck, and sweat squirting from its head in large drops.

'Do you know what a shell case is, Wil?' I ask, but Wil shakes his head.

Ellis described how, when marching past a row of small cottages, he'd seen an upturned shell case planted with flowers. Mam sighed, saying it was just typical of Ellis to notice small, irrelevant details like that, and to turn the sight into a symbol of hope.

We walk on silently. Wil's different, not at all himself. He's left school now, and is working with a carrier in the village, taking goods here and there. I'm contemplating how having to work probably changes a person. He has to keep his nose clean – people don't like busybodies. I take a sly look at him. I think his face has softened somehow: his nose not quite as sharp, it seems to me – not quite as rat-like. It's strange how all of us have changed – only months have passed since Lora and me would have hidden behind the wall, hurling stones and fir cones at him. I don't feel like throwing stones at anyone any more.

As we near the top of the hill, I can see someone rushing up the road towards us. It's Jim running up to me, with Lora following at a distance.

'Where are you off to, Jim?' I ask, as he grabs my hand, but I can't make out his answer. I wait for Lora.

'Where are you two going?' she asks, and I turn my back on Wil, as if to reassure Lora that I'm not accompanying him anywhere in particular.

'I'm going to fetch soap for Mam,' I say.

'I hope Ellis can stay in that place called Ro-Ro.' Wil turns to go.

'Rouen,' I nod, and he's gone.

'Will you come by my house?' Lora asks, and then she looks after Wil. 'What did he want?'

We both watch as Wil scuttles on. Back to the carrier, I expect – he has plenty of work to do.

'He was strange, Lora,' I say. 'He didn't want anything, and he didn't go on and on like he normally does, and he didn't even have any gossip to share... Very strange.'

Nothing seems as it used to be these days.

'How's your tada?' I ask.

'I suppose he's getting better,' she says. 'The scars are getting paler, and he ventures out into the back yard, but he comes straight back in if he thinks someone will see him there. He doesn't want anyone prying, and that's difficult because everyone's out and about in this fine weather, and Mam wants him out of the house. She can be quite peevish with him, too...' She takes Jim's hand, before adding, 'I can't work it out – I know it's difficult for Mam, but she's changed.'

She stops to adjust Jim's cap – it's covering his eyes. 'I had a real telling off yesterday, Anni. Well, you know how it is with Huw, but I decided to keep in touch with him, so I've been hiding notes – leaving them in a crack in the wall by the stile – and Mam found out.'

'How did she find that out?' I ask.

'It was Gwen Jones. She'd seen me putting one there, and had taken it out, and brought it straight to Mam.'

'Oh, Lora!' I gasp.

'Well, Mam got so mad at me, accusing me of all sorts. But, worst of all, telling me I was making it impossible for Tada to get better because I made him worry so much, thinking about me and Huw.' Lora's almost in tears, and I don't know what to say or how to comfort her.

'I don't know what to do, Anni. Do you think I'm to blame for Tada's slow progress in getting better?'

'Of course you aren't!' But I can't say anything else.

'And Jim won't go to Tada. He just rushes to me when Tada comes through, and hides his face in my skirt, and Mam says I spoil him.'

We're by the shop by now, and Lora stops to blow her nose furiously into her hanky. She gives me a crooked, sad little smile.

I push open the door, and the bell jingles as always. The blinds are down over the windows to protect the jars from the sun, so the shop feels nice and cool. I can hear Mrs Lloyd's measured footsteps coming from beyond the curtain.

'So it's you three little ones?' she greets us, with her usual warmth. 'Have you come to collect the soap, Anni?' and she glides back into the darkness through the curtain.

The bell jumps again as the door opens and a lady enters. I don't recognise her. Wisps of greying hair escape from under the brim of her straw hat, but I notice that her face is youngish – it doesn't match the greying hair, somehow. She jumps at the sound of the bell, and turns to squint up at the object that scared her. Her movements remind me of a small, nervous bird caught in a cage, willing the bars to open and release it. She raises one hand as if to steady her straw hat.

'Excuse me,' she stammers. 'I wonder if you can help me?'

Lora and I stare in her direction, but Jim's eyes are still fixed on the nearest sweet jar.

'I'm looking for someone,' she goes on. 'He lives in the village, but I don't know Trawsfynydd – I'm looking for a place called Tŷ'n Rhos.'

Lora steps forward.

'Tŷ'n Rhos?' says Lora.

'Yes, that's the name I have here. I'm looking for a gentleman called Ifor Edwards.'

'That's where I live,' Lora stammers, 'and Ifor Edwards is my father.'

I can tell that the strange woman is taken aback: she stands there, her fingers still holding on to the brim of her hat, staring at Lora. Then she coughs, nervously.

'Is your father at home?' she asks.

'Yes, we'll come with you now.' Lora grabs hold of Jim's hand and tugs him towards the door, but he struggles and starts to scream – he hasn't had his liquorice yet.

'Leave him with me, Lora,' I say. 'I'll bring him home.'

Lora leaves, taking the stranger to the house where Uncle Ifor will be hiding away in the back bedroom. Jim stops his screeching as Mrs Lloyd reaches for the liquorice jar.

18

Jim's happily chewing at his liquorice, and we both go down to throw pebbles into the stream. I don't want to take Jim back home yet. The strange woman's making me feel a little uneasy. What could she want with Uncle Ifor? I'll keep Jim with me for a while – having him back home wouldn't make anything easier. After messing about by the side of the stream for a while – till the splashing gets a little out of hand and Jim gets soaked – I decide to walk up towards the stile. We sit there and I collect pebbles for Jim. He places them on the rocks: crowding them into make-believe pens, turning them into his special flock of sheep. I'm always amazed at Jim's ability to play and amuse himself with little things. He can play for hours with just pebbles as imaginary sheep, herding them here and there along the edge of his mountain.

After a while, we climb the stile and slowly walk uphill towards Lora's house. When we're almost there, the strange woman appears again and passes us on her way. She's walking quickly, taking small, jerky steps, her eyes searching the road as if she's afraid of tripping. As she passes, she's muttering to herself, her breath coming in little gasps and her fingers fiddling with the ribbon at her neck. I don't think she notices us, because she doesn't look up.

By this point we've reached the street where Lora lives, and I turn to stare after the woman. A young man's appeared at her side, and she's leaning on his arm. Did she miss her step, I wonder, or has she been overcome by the heat? The young man turns towards us, and I realise it's Huw. I watch them go, the woman leaning heavily on his arm, and I gaze after them as they turn the corner.

I take Jim home, and Aunty Kitty grabs his hand.

'Thanks for having him, Anni,' she says distractedly, then adds, 'Come and have a cold drink before you turn for home.'

Lora hands me a mug of cool elderflower water, its sweetness filling my nose and making me feel a little queasy. In the chair in the far corner, his back to the window, sits Uncle Ifor. This is where he sits when he comes out of the back bedroom. He sits here because the curtain's partly drawn across the window, so there's always a shadow cast over him. The room seems always now to be draped in a shadow – it's not the light, welcoming place that Aunty Kitty always used to pride herself on keeping. Uncle Ifor sits there, completely still, his hands idle in his lap.

'But how did she know where to find you, Tada?' Lora asks. Her father sits, staring straight ahead.

'Tada?' Lora tries. Uncle Ifor looks over at Aunty Kitty, and she comes to him, placing a hand on his shoulder.

'Tada?' It's Lora again.

'Her husband was in the same battalion as your father, Lora,' Aunty Kitty starts. 'There was a young lad called Ted from Park Place in their battalion too, who your dad told me about in one of his letters. Well, Ted's home on leave now, and he went to see the lady, taking her some of her husband's things, you know. Ted told her about your father being one of the last people to see her husband... So she came to ask your father about him. Poor woman, she was shaken, seeing Ifor as he... well, as he is.'

Aunty Kitty pats Uncle Ifor's shoulder, as if she wants to reassure her husband that there's nothing to be shaken about.

'Did you know her husband, Tada?' Lora persists.

Uncle Ifor groans and nods.

'Yes, your father and her husband were close: they were friends. That's what worries your father, you see: they'd both been watching each other's backs while they were out there, and they were together in that bloody place – Mametz.'

'But how can you help, Tada? Mametz was where you were injured. How are you expected to remember anything about it? How can you tell her anything about her husband when you were so badly hurt?'

'She wasn't blaming your father for anything, Lora. She's just looking for answers, just as I would be – she just wants to hear from the last person to see her husband, I suppose, poor woman.'

Uncle Ifor looks up at his wife, gently placing his hand over hers. I can make out a muscle on his face twitching, as if he's willing words to form.

'O-Ow-Owen,' the name comes out, as if forced from a depth.

Jim's been sitting on my lap, fiddling with my hat.

'Owen Wills!' The words tumble out of Uncle Ifor's mouth.

We all stay completely still; not daring to breathe, almost. Uncle Ifor's strange voice resonates through the kitchen. It's Jim who breaks the stillness – dropping the hat, he laughs out loud. He gets off my knee and slowly ventures towards his father. Uncle Ifor doesn't know what to do at first, then he stoops forward and Aunty Kitty lifts Jim on to his father's knee. Uncle Ifor puts his arms around him, hugging his son to him. Then Aunty Kitty starts to laugh. She laughs and laughs, until eventually the laughter turns into silent sobs.

19

Dear family,

I'm writing hoping that you're all in good spirits and health, as I am. We've travelled for some days now, along roads and through countryside where the scars of war have left their ugly mark. Churches with their steeples destroyed, whole villages lying derelict and abandoned – but we march on, leaving France behind. We're now within the borders of Belgium.

I can't tell you our final position of course, or my letter will come to the attention of the officer, and be destroyed. But the place where we've set up camp can only be described as rather damp and uninviting: the ground seems to be waterlogged. The bombardment and the previous wet weather have turned the earth in places into a nasty-smelling bog, with deep crevasses filled with filthy water. In front of us is a canal, its water black and muddy, debris and empty Bully Beef cans floating along its surface. They tell me that we have to fetch our drinking water from it – I hope not! At any rate, I shall stay thirsty if that is the case, or else I shall have to break my temperance vow! One of the lads caught a rat in his kit bag last night... they're a plague. When we're still we can feel them scuttling over our limbs, or above our heads along the edge of the trench, sniffing. I then dream of being back home by the clear waters of the river, the stillness of the deep pools reflecting the light of the stars.

That's enough of my whining! Now I have a story for Enid and Anni – yesterday we were resting by the side of the road when a young lad came past leading two horses, one in each hand. One was a huge old shire, and the other a scraggy-looking gelding. I asked him about the horses and he turned and smiled.

'The two of them keep me going, you see,' he said. 'Now then, this one's called Little, and this one's Large, and the three of us get along very well. We carry the munitions to the trenches, and when it gets tough, I can rely on these two.'

He was a lad from Bala. There are so many soldiers here from North Wales – too many. Sometimes I wonder if anyone's still at home! It seems as if we're all outcasts here. Dear parents, try your hardest to keep Bob from having to come out here. Whatever it takes, he shouldn't have to come; and, God willing, the war will be over by the time Ifan's 18.

Father, I managed to finish the awdl, and it's been sent to be copied, and then hopefully it can be sent to the Eisteddfod competition. I don't know if it's up to scratch... or what will become of it. However, if the Eisteddfod asks for another awdl on the same title – 'Heroes' – for next year, then I have enough to write about now. I have seen many a hero out in these fields over the last few days. Not perhaps the toughest soldiers, but those men who manage to hold on to humanity and fraternity in the face of such darkness. They're the true heroes.

Thank you for the parcel, and the letters. Hearing from

you and about all the things you're up to, even little details, is such a comfort to me, so please keep the letters coming! Thanks for the cake, Maggie: it was delicious – although by the time it reached me, it was in pieces, with the parcels being thrown about. Try not to worry about me – you know how nimble I can be, I'll duck and run as best I can!

With warmest regards,
Your loving son and brother,
Ellis

It's Tada who reads Ellis's letter first. He reads it aloud and we all gather to listen, then Mam reads it for herself, and then each of us in turn. By the time Enid gets hold of it, its edges are tatty and the corners bent. Mam then puts it with all the others on the dresser, behind the family Bible. Sometimes neighbours and friends will call, and we hear about Ellis from letters sent to them. They're at a place called Ypres, we think – at least Tada says that's where they must be. Mr Thomas, the headmaster, let us have a look at the atlas the other day, although we're not at school now. He showed us where Belgium is, and where the front line passes. Lora says the front line's where the fighting happens, but I try not to think of that. I don't want to think of Ellis on the front line. So many of our boys have been stuck out in France for such a long time, and so many of them will stay there forever, under the sodden turf. It's a terrible place, so I try not to let the picture of it enter into my mind.

When his letters come, I instantly feel a weight lift. It's as if a little piece of Ellis returns with his letters and his voice comes to me, clear, just as if he was standing here telling us of his latest escapades.

It's late in the afternoon and Maggie's just returned from Blaenau Ffestiniog. She's been visiting Jini. Jini knows Ellis has managed to send his *awdl* in to the competition – she's pleased about it, and thinks he's got a good chance of winning. I hope so – he might be allowed home for the chairing ceremony. Jini's written to him, making him promise that he'll tell her if he's won, so that she can get herself a tidy hat. After all, she doesn't want to go with him to an important occasion like that in a scruffy old straw thing.

'A new hat!' Mam exclaims. 'We'll look swanky, won't we, all of us heading to Birkenhead on the train in borrowed hats? What would people say?'

I think she's secretly pleased and rather likes the idea, even though her voice has a slightly reprimanding tone to it. I don't think she'll be going to Birkenhead, but perhaps she'll lend Jini her fur stole.

On Sunday afternoon, I've promised to wait for Lora by the stile after chapel. The rest of the family have gone on ahead. Enid's a pain – sulking, wanting to stay with me – but I don't want her with me today. I need to see Lora: it's been a while. Thankfully, Maggie persuades Enid to go home with the promise that she'll help her make a dress for her doll.

Lora's late. I wait, but there's no sign of her. The weather's close and thundery, the heat forming a light haze which clings along the tops of the mountains. Just below, the heather's started to flower, turning the slopes a warm purple. It's quiet here. The sweet smell of the sun-drenched hay wafts on the breeze, but no one's working on the harvest today. It's Sunday and we're all busy praying, asking God for favours and making him listen to all our little worries. That's how it is here on a Sunday. Enid, Maggie and me went up to the mountain slopes to collect bilberries yesterday, and Mam made some jam. We want to send Ellis a jar, but it might break and then there'd be a terrible mess.

Then I see Lora. She's striding purposefully with Huw by her side, and my heart makes a lurch. I don't want to have to lie, or at least I don't want to have to tell half-truths, because Mam's bound to ask how Lora is and how she's feeling about not being allowed to see Huw. If I tell her I met up with Lora and Huw, then Aunty Kitty might find out. Also, I'd expected to have a good chat with Lora, and it's not the same when Huw's with us.

But as they approach, I notice Lora's face is flushed, her eyes glowing and excited. She rushes down the last bit of the hill, throwing herself on to the grass beside me. Huw hangs back, as if he knows I don't really want him there.

'Anni,' Lora catches her breath. 'Anni, I've got news.'

'Oh?'

'Anni – remember the lady who came to see us?'

'The one we met in the shop?' I ask.

'Yes. Well, who do you think she is?' Lora's plucking at the grass.

I can't imagine who she might be, other than the fact she's Owen Wills wife, but I've only heard of him because of Uncle Ifor's letter. I don't actually know him. Huw comes and sits silently on the stile step. Laura glances up at him and smiles.

'Well – she's Huw's mother.'

'Your mother?' I ask, and Huw gives me a small smile, as if to apologise for the mystery.

'Yes – Mam.' His voice is low. 'She found out Lora's father was with my father at Mametz. My father was Owen Williams – people called him Owen Wills. They were friends.'

I can make out the sadness in Huw's voice, and in the way he said Owen Wills *was* his father. He once had a father. His mother once had a husband, who loved and cared for her and their young family. That was before the war came.

Then Lora tugs at my arm – she has more news, it seems.

'Do you remember the letter Tada wrote to Mam?' she asks. I'm a little cross – of course I remember the wretched letter. How could I forget? The words of that letter still haunt me, often at night, when the stars disappear.

'Well, in it Tada writes about Owen Wills, his friend and Huw's father. Well, the reason Tada didn't want me to see Huw was because he felt guilty, you see.'

'But why?' I don't understand. 'Why should Uncle Ifor feel bad? He did nothing to be ashamed of, did he? There was nothing he could have done.'

'No, there was nothing he could have done,' Huw nods sadly. 'Mam knows that, and wanted to reassure Lora's father.'

'So why did Uncle Ifor not want you to see Huw, then, Lora?' I ask, confused.

'Tada had worked it out. He knew Huw was Owen Wills's son because they'd talked so often about their families – about us. It was a comfort to them when they were waiting in the trenches.' Lora smiles shyly. 'Owen Wills had talked so often about his clever son.'

Huw laughs, as Lora goes on.

'Tada had promised Owen he'd get him home somehow, but he failed, didn't he? He just couldn't do it – he failed to keep his promise, and that will always haunt him.'

'I suppose I was a reminder, wasn't I?' Huw whispered. 'When I came to Trawsfynydd, I opened the can of worms again. When he realised I was Owen Wills's son. Of course he didn't want me near Lora. He was struggling to shove the whole thing as far as he could to the back of his mind – he had enough to get on with, rebuilding his life, trying to come to terms with that wound... he didn't want me around him.'

My mind was racing, trying to understand it all.

'So Aunty Kitty knew who Huw was?' I try, staring at Lora, and she nodded.

'Yes, they'd both worked out who I was.' Huw paused, picking some lichen off the wall. 'But sometimes you can't keep promises

– not the impossible ones anyway – and it isn't your fault when that happens.'

'Tada understands that now, after your mother's visit, doesn't he? And he's happy for you to come and call for me.' Lora stands.

'I wish Mam could accept that my father's not coming back. I thought perhaps seeing your father, Lora, would help,' Huw adds. 'But it hasn't. She still thinks he's out there somewhere. She refuses to put his things away: his shoes are still waiting by the back door, his coat on the peg. She goes out to his workshop to tidy his tools, but she only moves them about, because they don't need tidying, do they? The chisel lies there idle, as always. And she spends so much time just staring at the chair where he used to sit.'

No one speaks. I can't get rid of the image of the strange, bird-like woman flitting around, tidying and cleaning a workshop, hovering around the apparition of a lost husband.

'There's no body to grieve over, no grave...' Huw's voice is so quiet I hardly hear his words. 'She's off to London tomorrow. An official's agreed to meet her, to look into our case. But we'd have heard if he'd been taken prisoner, or if he was in hospital.' He looks at Lora, and then at me. 'Wouldn't we?'

Lora nods.

I don't know what to say. Then Lora smiles, a sudden lightness crossing her face.

'Come on, then,' she says. 'Come with us for tea, Anni. Huw's coming, and Mam's baked a tart, and we have cream.'

But we're subdued. We're all lost in our own thoughts.

20

Mam's just like a clucking hen. She wants us all around her all the time, not happy if any of us is out of her sight. It's all the news from the front: it's in the local paper now, reports of the fighting in Flanders. Those who seem to know say it's fierce. They're calling this the Third Battle of Ypres, because that's where the fighting's happening, and it's the third time that village has been in the middle of things. The papers have reported on a push to take a place called Passchendaele from the Germans. One of the papers said that the Welsh Fusiliers had taken a major part in the fighting there on the last day of July, and it was a plan thought out by a very important officer called Haig. I just hope this very important officer is also very clever, because Ellis is in that regiment. But Bob doesn't think much of this Haig man, because Bob says officers like Haig don't do the fighting themselves, they just plan it. I hope Haig's plan worked, anyway.

Tada reads the paper, and I hear him tell Mam the war's going well for our boys: they've taken land from the Germans. Mam tells Tada she doesn't believe anything the papers say any more. She thinks it's all lies, because they need more men to join up. Mam says of course the number of soldiers lost is high, but the papers won't report on that – they have to be positive. The only thing I know is that we haven't had a letter from Ellis recently. All of us jump when we hear the postman's footsteps, expectant, but no one mentions the lack of letters.

The days slip by, and we wait, mulling over any little thread of news. Other families with sons in the same regiment have received letters, but no one makes a song and dance over them.

Trawsfynydd has fallen silent and we all pray, trying to cheer each other on, with hope and fear washing over us simultaneously. Sometimes one of my brothers will come home from the village having heard something – only rumours – but they seem sometimes like a cold breeze forewarning of a change in the weather. The waiting's taking its toll on Tada and Mam: I hear them whispering through the wooden partition when we're lying in bed, and in the morning I know from Mam's face that sleep didn't come.

I've been to the village. It's my turn to collect donations so the Sunday School can send money overseas where people don't have shoes, and haven't heard about Jesus either. I asked the minister if the Germans had heard about Jesus, and he said they had. I don't understand it. This country knows everything about Jesus too, just like the Germans, but we all fight anyway.

I go to collect Gwen Jones's donation. I stand on the step outside her door – no one ever gets invited into Gwen Jones's house.

'Have you heard from Ellis?' she asks. Everyone asks me that.

'No, not yet,' I reply.

'No?' Brows raised, face accusing, her sharp eyes searching my face. Thankfully, she doesn't wear the fox fur in the house.

'No, we haven't had a letter for some time now – well, since the last week in July.' I know that, because it's mid-August now. Three weeks have passed.

'Strange,' she says, and adds, 'I've heard that a special someone has had a letter from him.'

She pauses then, as if to see what reaction her words will have on me. I don't know what to say, so I just stand there on the doorstep, staring at her.

'Well, that's what I heard, anyway.' She clears her throat, and goes on. 'Someone I know was in Blaenau yesterday, and spoke to that lady friend of his... Oh, I don't remember her name.'

'Jini Owen?' I whisper. Has Jini had a letter? *Dear Lord, make it be true. Please Lord, make it be true that Jini's got a letter from him, telling her he's fine. I promise I'll...*

I've started praying again, praying with my eyes open, because I can't take them off Gwen Jones's face. She's smiling at me, as if I amuse her.

'Ah, yes, that's it: Jini Owen.' But she doesn't go on, and I have to know.

'What did the letter say, Mrs Jones?' I blurt. 'Is Ellis safe?' My throat's bone dry.

'Goodness! I haven't a clue what he told her, but isn't just knowing that a letter has come enough to prove that he's well?' she replies, and I nod. 'But you didn't get a letter from him, then?' she queries again, her eyes narrow. I can't answer her, so I just shake my head, turn on my heel and flee.

I run until I reach the bridge, then I have to stop to catch my breath. I lean over the parapet.

Dear Lord up in Heaven, I promise to give Enid all of my worldly treasures, including the brooch, my red ribbon and my collection of quartz stones. I promise to fetch water without being asked, and to clean out the hen coop every week. I promise to pray, I promise not to join in the racket at the Band o'Hope... if only You will bring Ellis safely home.

I must have been praying out loud, because all of a sudden Wil's there by my side, and he's looking at me oddly.

'Are you all right, Anni?' he asks. 'Who were you talking to?' He looks about him, and then over the parapet, as if expecting to see someone hiding there.

'I was just singing,' I try.

'Oh! There you are then.' He doesn't question me. 'On your way home, are you?'

'Yes.'

'How are you all, Anni?' he asks.

'Fine, thank you.' But Wil just nods, his face grave.

'You'd better get on home, Anni,' he says, smiles wanly, then hurries off.

Aunty Kitty's with Mam in the kitchen when I get home. Mam's sitting by the table, and suddenly I realise that she looks old. Dark shadows stain the skin beneath her eyes. Of course, Aunty Kitty's so much younger than her – only in her thirties, not that much older than our Ellis. Lora's her eldest, and Enid and I are the youngest of Mam and Tada's children. It's why Mam seems suddenly old to me, I try to reason.

Aunty Kitty smiles when she sees me.

'Here she is,' she laughs. Has Mam been worried about me?

I nod at them and rush to fetch the water buckets. I have a promise to keep.

'Did you see Lora in the village?' Aunty Kitty asks, and I shake my head. 'You haven't heard the news, then?' she goes on.

'No, what news?'

'Huw's had good news!' she laughs, and Mam smiles. 'Did you know his mother went down to London?'

'Yes,'

'Well, the authorities – well, an officer or someone, made enquiries on their behalf and...'

'Yes?' I put the buckets down.

'They think they've found Owen Wills!'

'But how?'

'Well, there's a patient, a soldier, in a military hospital down in the south of England – I can't remember the name of the place. This patient, well, he can only say that his name's Owen. He can't remember any English, can only remember how to speak Welsh – they think it's the shock, or a head injury, perhaps... Anyway, Huw's mother's on her way there.'

'Isn't that sort of good news, Anni?' Mam tries. I know what

Mam means, but Aunty Kitty seems to think it's wonderful news, so I try and smile at her.

'How's Ifor taking it?' Mam asks.

'He's so glad – we all are. We're all praying things will turn out well for them.'

Then Mam remembers my errand.

'Did you collect all the missionary money, Anni? How was Gwen Jones?'

'Yes, Mam. Mrs Jones was fine.' But I don't tell her about the letter. I don't need to, because Maggie comes in, and Jini's with her. They're both excited and in high spirits.

'Mam, Mam!' Maggie calls from the door.

'Is that Jini?' Mam rises and makes room for her by the table.

'Look what Jini got!' Maggie takes the letter from Jini's hand, and places it on the table.

We all crowd over the letter. It has a poem in it, scrawled in Ellis's hand. It's a poem to wish Jini a happy birthday – her twenty-seventh birthday.

'Read it, Mam,' Maggie urges.

'No, Maggie: it's Jini's letter. We shouldn't pry.' She looks at Jini shyly, and a blush deepens on Jini's cheeks. A look passes between the two, a look that says: *There you are, Jini: I hand my son over to you now. He's yours to love and cherish – take good care of him.*

But I've already had a glimpse of the letter.

It's then that I remember about the water buckets. I leave everyone in the kitchen, talking about the miraculous discovery of Owen Wills, and the wonder of Ellis' letter to his sweetheart. Was it just me who'd noticed the smudge of a date at the top of the page? Or was it that they didn't want to see it? The date was 29 July. Two days before the battle we'd read about, the battle where Ellis's regiment had fought.

I'm struggling back with the full buckets when Aunty Kitty and Jini meet me in the front yard, on their way back towards the village.

'Come over soon, Anni. Lora will want to tell you all about Huw's father, I expect!'

I smile and they leave, a lightness in both their steps.

I turn to pick up the buckets again. Enid's standing in the doorway. I call her to help me, but she's looking away down the road, then she turns and rushes inside. I put down the buckets again and run to the gate – what did she see? I can't see anyone, but above, over towards the river I can hear a buzzard mewing, and another answering its call. Was that it? I watch the two buzzards circling ahead: round and round they glide, watching their prey. Suddenly they swoop, and a cold shiver takes hold of me, the August heat evaporating.

Then I see the messenger. I watch as Tada walks to meet him, greeting him quietly. I watch Tada's face change as he reaches for the small envelope the man's holding out for him. The man turns, his head bowed, and I watch as he walks slowly down the lane. Tada waits before opening the envelope; he reads; and I watch as he slumps and leans heavily on the gate. There before my eyes, my father turns into a frail, broken man.

*

There are no more words to be said. Yr Ysgwrn is a house of sorrow. Mam's gone to bed – she went up straight away, and I don't know when she'll venture down again. Tada's sat all day at the kitchen table, the Bible in front of him, but the words unread. He hasn't been able to open the book. It's dark now, and Enid and I are in bed. The others stay up to keep Tada company, not wanting to leave him there, but no one speaks. Enid comes up close to me, but tonight I don't shove her away over to her side of the bed. Instead I put my arms around her, and hold her tightly. I stroke her hair. The sobbing's turned to little groans, but at least she's asleep now. Gently I release her, tucking the bedclothes around her. I get up, and part the curtains so that I can look up at the sky. The fine weather's breaking at last. The sky's overcast, there are no stars, and I know tonight in that place called Ypres, all will be dark.

September 1918

I OFTEN GO into the little parlour where the chair stands. It's the Chair from the National Eisteddfod at Birkenhead. Ellis's *awdl* was awarded the highest prize. He'd won, but he wasn't there to collect it. None of us went there that day. It's a tall, heavy chair, its dark wood a tangle of fancy carvings. It's a beautiful chair, I suppose, but no one ever sits in it. We call it the black chair.

Today though, I go into the parlour to fetch my best dress. It's an old dress of Maggie's, the one she got made for her in Liverpool, but she's cleverly altered it, sewing a fine lace collar on to it for me. Mam's been over it with the iron, carefully, pressing the lace collar, so it's been allowed to be laid out on the chair to stop it from creasing again.

Today's the wedding day of Lora Margaret and Huw Williams. Lora's asked me to be bridesmaid. Aunty Kitty and Uncle Ifor will be there at the chapel, and Huw's mother, and his father – Owen Wills – is coming. As soon as he was well enough, he came to meet Uncle Ifor. Lora says there wasn't a dry eye in their house that day, when the two saw for themselves that both really had somehow managed to get out of the hell that was Mametz.

After the chapel service, Nain and Aunty Kitty have prepared a tea at Lora's house. Mam's made a currant loaf – I must remember to take it with me.

I'm dressed now, and Maggie's taken the rags out of my hair. They all smile, and Mam says I look a picture. I think the curls make me look older, somehow.

'Wait!' Enid jumps down the stairs, the red ribbon in her hand. Maggie clips it in my hair.

'Is it you that's getting married?' Tada smiles quietly. I spin, and the dress swirls. Even Ifan smiles at me, and says I look 'alright'.

Before I start for the lane, Mam opens the Bible and gets a paper out. I can see it's a poem, in Ellis's hand. It's the poem 'Gwenfron and I'.

'Take it.' Mam puts it into an envelope, and hands it to me. I know she's trying to be brave. 'Give it to Lora and Huw, will you, Anni? Tell them that we all send our best wishes.'

Mam goes through to the parlour, and I place the poem on top of the currant loaf in the basket. Mam's standing by the chair, the black chair. I know the chair will stay in Yr Ysgwrn as long as our family's here. It'll always remind us of Hedd Wyn, the poet, but mostly it'll remind us of Ellis – our special Ellis, and all the other sons, lovers, husbands and brothers that have been lost. It will be here – an empty chair, like so many other empty chairs.

The sun's lower in the sky, but its warmth promises an Indian summer, the heather flowering a warm pink on the slopes. I stand on the front step. I have a wedding to attend. It's then that I spot the sparkling edge of a small quartz stone sticking out of the dirt. I dig it out, rubbing it carefully in the grass, getting the soil out of the cracks. I might just keep it in my pocket, because if I don't keep it, then...

I look up, and Mam's there in the parlour window, watching me. She smiles, but gently shakes her head. I drop the stone. It settles in the dirt, and I remember the quartz ring Lora conjured up on that day by the stile, when she dreamed of marrying Lloyd George's son. I smile at Mam. Lora won't need a quartz stone to bring her luck today.

Also from Y Lolfa:

£12.99

y Lolfa

THE FOLLOW-UP TO THE NUMBER ONE
BESTSELLER, *THE WELSH AT MAMETZ WOOD*

The Welsh at
PASSCHENDAELE
— 1917 —

DR JONATHAN HICKS

£14.99

An Empty Chair is just one of a whole range of publications from Y Lolfa. For a full list of books currently in print, send now for your free copy of our new full-colour catalogue. Or simply surf into our website

www.ylolfa.com

for secure on-line ordering.

TALYBONT CEREDIGION CYMRU SY24 5HE
e-mail ylolfa@ylolfa.com
website www.ylolfa.com
phone (01970) 832 304
fax 832 782